Take the Motherhood Challenge:

- Do the colors pink and blue make tears well up in your eyes?

- Do you feel compelled to soothe and cuddle every crying baby you see?

- Are you always volunteering to change your best friend's baby's diaper—just to get some quality time in with the cute little tot?

- Does the sight of a handsome man with a baby make your ring finger itch?

If you answered yes to one or more of these questions, you better get yourself in the family way—fast! Of course, if you just so happen to meet a hunk with a baby, you could find yourself on the road to marriage and motherhood sooner than you think....

Dear Reader,

I think we all remember the story of Aladdin and his lamp, and I'm willing to bet we've all had a few moments in life when we wished we owned that lamp. Really, how hard would it be for me to become tall, thin and so gorgeous that the man of my dreams (who keeps changing on an almost-daily basis, of course) couldn't possibly resist me? Impossible without the lamp, but with it…? Who knows! In Alice Sharpe's *If Wishes Were Heroes* there is indeed such a lamp, or at least there seems to be. Whether it's magical or not, it certainly succeeds in bringing Gina Cox and Alan Kincaid together, and isn't that really the point?

Popular Christie Ridgway is back with *Have Baby, Will Marry*. All Molly Michaels set out to find was a dog. Her friends were all having babies, but for Molly, playing single mom to a cuddly canine was enough. Until she discovered that said canine came attached to gorgeous Weaver Reed and tiny, adorable Daisy. Suddenly, walking the dog looked a whole lot less appealing than walking straight into Weaver's embrace—marriage-of-convenience proposal and all!

I think you're going to love both these books, and I hope you'll rejoin us next month for two more lighthearted tales about unexpectedly meeting, dating—and marrying!—Mr. Right.

Leslie Wainger

Leslie Wainger
Senior Editor and Editorial Coordinator

Please address questions and book requests to:
Silhouette Reader Service
U.S.: 3010 Walden Ave., P.O. Box 1325, Buffalo, NY 14269
Canadian: P.O. Box 609, Fort Erie, Ont. L2A 5X3

CHRISTIE RIDGWAY

Have Baby, Will Marry

SILHOUETTE YOURS TRULY™

Published by Silhouette Books
America's Publisher of Contemporary Romance

Thank you to critique partners past and present:
Caro, Joyce, Judith, Judy, Marsha, Maureen and Terry.

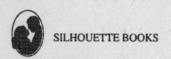 SILHOUETTE BOOKS

ISBN 0-373-52051-4

HAVE BABY, WILL MARRY

Copyright © 1997 by Christie Ridgway

About the author

CHRISTIE RIDGWAY fell in love with romance novels as a girl, when she spent all her allowance money on romances and red licorice vines. Now she fulfills her dream of being a published author in Southern California. Work time is only occasionally (hah!) interrupted by her two young sons. In addition to writing, she volunteers at her children's school and loves to read and cook.

Christie credits her happiness to the smarts she used in picking her husband of twelve-plus years, Rob.

Books by Christie Ridgway

Silhouette Yours Truly

1

Molly Michaels let herself into her vacationing parents' home and heaved a gusty sigh of relief. Free at last! She'd made a successful, that is, early, escape from her twelfth—no, thirteenth—baby shower in six months. With a flick of her wrist, she tossed the mail and the flyer she'd found beneath the welcome mat onto the kitchen table.

Five years ago her calendar had overflowed with bridal showers. Now all of her friends seemed to be having babies. And while she loved the little sweethearts—even was godmother to two of them—tiny sleepers, tiny shoes, the *oohs* and *aahs* over piles of tiny items made her—

The phone rang before she could describe the sensation.

"Are you okay?" her best friend Dana demanded.

"Fine." Molly ignored Dana's obvious concern and began sorting the mail.

"You didn't even stay long enough for cake."

"You know I'm cured of chocolate. Besides, I had a headache."

"Pink and blue seem to do that to you lately," Dana said. "That was your excuse at the last shower we went to."

Molly didn't want to examine the issue. "Mmm. Is that the baby I hear crying in the background?" She stacked the long envelopes in one pile and the short envelopes in another. "I expect you to hop to it when my goddaughter wants her mommy."

"I know what you're doing."

Mail sorted by size, Molly considered a second sort by color. Then her gaze snagged on the neon green flyer that lay beneath the envelopes. "What am I doing? I'll give you three guesses." Like a magician with a tablecloth, she jerked out the flyer. The envelope stacks toppled.

"You're moping over witless and wandering Jonathon."

Molly stared at the blank back of the flyer, waiting for a twinge of pain. She smiled when it didn't happen. "Nope."

"You're wishing you were a newlywed instead of a newly free."

Not even a ghost of regret for the unused wedding gown hanging in her closet. "Wrong again." Idly, she flipped over the flyer.

"You're wanting a baby."

Molly sucked in a breath. *Don't admit to it*, a self-protective instinct screamed, and her hand tightened on the bilious green flyer. She squeezed shut her eyes, then opened them and relaxed her grip on the paper.

"You there?" Dana asked.

Molly smoothed out the sheet against the counter-top, wishing she could smooth away her urges for something warm and cuddly with as much ease. She stared at the paper. Everything Must Go! blazed in inch-high letters across the top, followed by a list of household equipment.

Her gaze drifted down. In smaller type, another headline, Free To A Good Home, stretched above a photo of a medium-sized, medium-type dog. Floppy ears. Someone with a sense of humor had drawn a cartoon bubble beside the animal. "Take me, I'm yours!" it woofed through a goofy, doggy grin.

Dog. Warm and cuddly.

Dana's voice penetrated her thoughts. "What *are* you doing?"

Molly stared at the paper. She was twenty-nine years old, and even without a mate in her life, the baby urges kept coming hard and fast. Was this a happy substitute? "I'm thinking about getting a dog," she said slowly. "Warm and cuddly, no man neces-sary."

Weaver Reed stepped over the spotted dog, Patch, settled gingerly in a chair, then quickly punched the series of numbers to connect him to the Maryland headquarters of XNS, the private company of ex-military intelligence officers he worked for.

At the tinny click of connection, Weaver impa-tiently stabbed out another sequence to put him through to his partner. XNS handled everything from tracing laundered money to negotiating hostage releases, and if he'd wanted to get deeper into the organization, his voice would have gone through security's print analysis. But in another moment he reached his party.

"Gabe Morgan."

"Gabe, it's Weaver. Did you find someone, somewhere, related to me?" From another part of the house, a little noise made Weaver jump guiltily. "Tell me what you got and tell me quick."

"You, uh, free?"

Weaver cut his gaze in the direction of the hall. "For the moment. What've you got?" he repeated softly.

"I'm still working on it," Gabe answered.

"Still working on it!" Weaver ground the words out. "You've had a full month, Gabe."

"Yeah, yeah, yeah." Amusement laced the other man's voice. "But you know how much I hate desk duty."

Weaver throttled the phone receiver. "So you think being bad at it means you'll have to do it less often?"

"A guy can hope."

Weaver took a deep breath. "You don't have anything?"

"Your family leaves lousy tracks."

My parents were damn good at sneaking off, that's for sure. "We're not talking about the Rockefellers, Gabe. We're looking for some descendants of a dirt-

poor, uneducated branch of backwoods trash, okay?"
He rubbed a hand down his face. "God, *somebody*
must be left and have turned out all right. And if not
a Reed, then someone on her mother's side."

"You're sounding a little desperate, buddy."

"Wouldn't you be?" Weaver shot back. "Until I
find some responsible and willing member of the family, I'm stuck in the 'burbs of San Diego. Hell, just a
month ago we were planning the job in the Czech
Republic. Two months ago I was belly-crawling
through the jungle in Central America."

"My heart bleeds." Gabe laughed without sympathy. "What's wrong with the suburbs, anyhow?"

"I'm in 'em, that's what. Dammit, Gabe, I feel like
a fish gulping for air on the sand."

Gabe laughed again. "Yeah, but you have your
beautiful partner."

Weaver groaned loudly, then immediately cut himself off as another sound floated down the hall.

"Where is the gorgeous Daisy Ann, by the way?"

"Sleeping, I hope," Weaver said. "And that might
last only minutes, so give it to me straight, Gabe.
Nothing? You've found nothing?"

"Well—"

A piercing racket obliterated the rest of Gabe's answer. Weaver squeezed shut his eyes. "Wait, wait. I
think she's awake."

"You *think?* I can hear her all the way to Maryland. Get that woman who's supposed to be looking
after her."

Cordless phone to his ear, Weaver headed down the hall toward the source of the noise. "The woman left. Another offer, a permanent offer, came through. What could I say?" The noise was so loud now that Weaver could feel the membranes of his inner ears shuddering in distress. He paused at an ajar door.

After a brief hesitation, he palmed it all the way open. The crying stopped immediately. Fluffy clouds and Little Boy Blue sheep floated into his vision. The unmistakable aroma of a dirty diaper assailed his nose.

"Can you smell *that* all the way to Maryland?"

Gabe laughed, too uproariously, Weaver thought as he pinched the phone between his ear and shoulder and picked up his smelly "partner." She blinked tear-drenched lashes and smiled at him as if he were a full stomach and a warm bath rolled into one.

Which of course he was—now that the nanny had gone.

Daisy Ann butted her head in a baby cuddle against his shoulder. Weaver ignored the small clenching pain it caused in the vicinity of his chest.

A man like me has nothing to offer a kid.

"Tell me you found somebody to take her, Gabe," he said desperately.

"Sorry, ol' buddy. So far, I've found nothing. *Nada.* Zippo."

In her old bedroom at her parents'—Molly's temporary headquarters until her small house in a nearby tract was completed—she changed from a dress to her summer uniform of shorts and a T-shirt. With practiced movements, she braided her long dark hair, then walked outside with the bright green flyer in hand. The address on the paper seemed familiar.

As she turned the corner, she recognized a house halfway down the block. A childhood buddy had once lived there and it hadn't changed over the years. Perched on the edge of a canyon, the house was large, Spanish-style, with a sloping front lawn and a huge California pepper tree.

The amazing number of For Sale signs posted around the place were new. Poked in the lawn. Pasted on two cars in the driveway. Leaning against a set of tools: lawn mower, weed whapper, leaf blower. Everything about the place shouted *Moving on.*

Molly trekked up the terra-cotta tile steps to the front porch. The wooden door stood open, a heavy screen door fuzzing her view of the dim inside. The doorbell made a muted *dong* that set off an immediate scrabbling of claws against wooden floors. In seconds, Molly was nose to nose with her baby substitute.

"Hey, you—girl, uh, boy." From her vantage behind the screen door, it was hard to tell the gender of the black-and-white canine.

The dog grinned, the same smile that had caught her attention on the flyer.

"You're a friendly pup." Molly peered through the screen down the dark hall, searching for signs of other occupants. "You home alone, good dog?"

Thwap, thwap, thwap. The dog turned in the direction she looked, its tail slamming the screen.

Molly pushed the bell again. Again the muted sound. The dog turned back to stare at her and cocked its head as if to say, *Hey, what do you want? I'm here already.*

Shaking her head, Molly smiled. "I see you, pup." She stood for a few minutes on the porch, alternately listening for sounds of life from the house and carrying on a conversation with the dog.

"Would you like a new home?" she asked.

With you? she imagined its smile was saying. *Absolutely!*

"I have a yard, quite a bit of free time and only a few requirements."

The dog continued grinning. *Name them!*

"You'll be loyal? No broken promises?"

The dog sat. *None.*

"No grousing about which video I rent? Doesn't have to have T and A or the Terminator?"

Another wide smile. *The important thing is we'll be watching it together.*

"No looking at younger owners with bigger you-know-whats?"

The dog's head cocked left. *I thought you wanted a baby substitute, not something better than a man.*

Molly grimaced with chagrin, looking into sympathetic canine eyes. "Smart aleck. But I haven't gotten to the warm and cuddly part yet."

"I'm listening."

Molly started. While she'd been preoccupied with her imaginary discussion with the dog, someone had come into the entryway. A big, dark, dangerously handsome someone.

Six-two or six-three. Close-cropped dark hair, a ruggedly planed face, dimple slashes in his cheeks.

In the surprised silence, the dog whined.

Molly felt a little like doing that herself. Because Mr. Big-and-Just-the-Type-She-Liked was obviously attached. *Significantly* attached. Straining across his broad chest were the straps of an incongruously feminine baby carrier. Over his heart sat the pack itself, with a pair of floppy baby legs poking out. She could see the top of a little head and one relaxed hand.

"Sorry it took so long to get to the door," the great-looking man said. "But now that I'm here, well, hi." He smiled, and the dimple slashes deepened.

Unable to help herself, she smiled back.

Warmth entered his blue eyes, a warmth that sent little tingles through the air to land on her skin. *Ooooh.* Molly blinked at the feeling, trying to clear her head. He was looking at her in a familiar way, but it didn't seem right somehow. Something was wrong....

His smile widened even further. "Tongue-tied?" he prompted. His gaze flicked over her again, all hot zips and zaps.

And then she realized what wasn't right. *He was looking at her as if he were single!*

She crossed her arms over her chest and frowned.

"I saw the flyer." Her voice came out crisp and businesslike.

"The flyer." His smile, that *I'm single* smile didn't dim.

Molly's teeth ground together. Didn't he get it? Didn't he realize that an attached man—attached and a father, of all things!—shouldn't look at another woman like this? In a way that made her hot on the outside and itchy on the inside?

"Maybe adopting a dog isn't such a good idea after all," she said, not wanting to involve herself with a sleaze like this guy. She stepped back, though she didn't have the guts to look at the dog.

The man's smile faded. "You want to adopt Patch?" He pushed open the screen, and both he and the animal bounded out. "Don't change your mind!"

The anxious note in his voice made her pause. Maybe she'd been hasty. Maybe she'd misread the man's gaze. Molly looked down at the dog, Patch.

It leaned against her leg, imploring her with its eyes. *Give us a chance.*

Weaver couldn't believe he'd almost blown it. The first person to show the least bit of interest in something he needed to get rid of, and he'd been so busy admiring her great—everything—he'd nearly scared her off.

She knelt to pet the dog—good boy, Patch—and he got a few more moments of free admiring time. Her long legs folded beneath her and he followed the sleek line of her dark braid.

"Male?" She turned her head toward him. Wide, silvery gray eyes regarded him coolly. Except that the eyes reminded him of a baked Alaska—cold ice cream wrapped in an otherwise hot package. "Male?" she asked again.

He smiled, because everything about her pleased him. Baked Alaska, he thought again, chuckling to himself. Hot and cold and sweet, sweet, sweet. Male? "You betcha."

"Neutered?"

He was deep in ice-cream fantasies. "No way, honey."

She rose abruptly. "Pardon me?" Now the voice was as cool as the eyes.

Weaver hastily collected himself. "No, no. Pardon *me*. You're talking about Patch?" *Of course she's talking about Patch, you fool.* "Neutered."

He remembered he was supposed to be selling here. "Two years old. Good with kids." He smiled at her again and sidled closer. "You have kids?" She didn't wear a ring, and if she was as unattached as he was, maybe they could get together, have a few laughs…

Her cool eyes were on him again. "No. *I* don't have any children." She focused on his chest. Weaver forced himself not to take an overly deep breath, but he was glad for his disciplined regimen of weights. He vowed to add ten more reps at the bench press.

He started working up to the date question. "Uh, well—"

"So it looks like you're planning on moving," she said, rising.

Weaver caught another full-force view of her legs. In a blinding flash, he realized he was a leg man. Long, muscular runner's legs. "What makes you say that?" *Her* legs.

"Might be all the For Sale signs."

"Oh. Yeah." He snapped to attention. No more goofs. One, get her to take the dog, he ordered himself. Two, get her to go out with him. "Patch needs a home."

"Doesn't seem like he's a barker."

"That's right. He's great. Quiet. Likes to go for walks." He smiled just a bit, to show her he was kidding around. "Kind of like me."

She stared at his chest again. "Oh, really." No answering smile.

"I'm Weaver, by the way. Weaver Reed." He held out his hand.

"Molly Michaels." Her fingers, long and slender, came toward his reluctantly.

Bam! Her hand slid into his and he felt it like a hammer blow to the head. She retreated quickly, but not before he saw the recognition in that silver gaze. Chemistry. Pure sizzle and fire. She knew it, too.

Nothing ventured, nothing gained, he encouraged himself. "Could we get together sometime?" He wouldn't be around for long. "Soon?"

Her eyes widened. Her lips pursed, then thinned to a disapproving line. "No, thank you."

"Ah." It had been years since he'd been this disappointed. Not since that first couple at the family services agency had decided against adopting him. "Boyfriend? Husband?"

She stared at his face, his chest, his face again. "Wife? Child?" she said, as if he were an idiot.

Now his eyes widened. He could feel air hitting newly exposed whites. "Wife? Child?" he repeated.

Her expression matched his puzzlement. "What's her name?" she asked abruptly.

"Her name?" he repeated again. Who was she talking about?

She gestured toward his chest, which she'd seemed so fascinated with earlier.

Weaver looked down. And then he felt the flush rush across his face. He wasn't a stupid man, really. But she was an exceptionally beautiful woman, and he just hadn't been thinking straight. Thinking at all.

He'd forgotten all about Daisy Ann.

He'd thought a whole slew of other dumb things.

"Oh, God," he said. *A comment sure to up your intelligence in her estimation, Reed.* "Let me explain," he started, then broke off, unsure how to begin.

"I'm listening."

He noticed her toe was tapping, too, so he jumped into the middle of the story before her patience evaporated. "I inherited all this." He waved his arms to indicate the house and the cars. "Guardianship of the baby, too."

Her gaze left his face and traveled down to the snoozing Daisy Ann.

Weaver cupped the baby's downy head with his palm. "She's only four months old." *And I promise she'll have a family.* No way would she grow up in foster homes the way he had.

"Inherited from whom?" Creases of concern lined Molly's forehead.

"From my cousin and his wife. I'd only met him once. He tracked me down about fourteen years ago."

"And he left you everything? Including his baby?" She shook her head. "I don't get it."

"Jim and his wife were killed in a light plane crash." He stroked the baby's head. "I was named in their will."

Surprise showed all over her face. "Why you? No offense, but if he'd only met you once…"

He nodded, understanding her shock. Hell, he'd nearly had a heart attack when he'd found out. "We'd exchanged letters over the years, and Jim and Ellen were big on family ties. They'd met in an orphanage. I was Jim's only family." Like Weaver, they'd played the please-won't-somebody-adopt-me game. Like Weaver, no one ever had.

He looked down at Daisy's head. *But I'll find two parents for you. A real family.* "And now I'm selling everything off to put in trust for Daisy Ann."

Molly didn't seem to be in a hurry anymore. He went on to tell her he had a job in Maryland. Not *what* he did, but just that he was heading back to the

East Coast as soon as possible. And because he didn't want to get into talking about his job or his background, he didn't tell her he had to find someone else to adopt Daisy Ann.

As he suspected, Molly Michaels was a kind woman. She remained cool, maybe even cooler once she heard he was intent on returning to Maryland, but she volunteered to take Patch. She was a first-grade teacher, living in her parents' house just around the corner until September.

Yeah, a nice lady. She touched a gentle finger to Daisy Ann's hair when she left. Patch looked sort of anxious but consented to being led off without a whimper.

After they'd walked out of sight, Weaver remembered a million things he wished he'd told her. That Patch liked the kind of food with the chuck wagon on the package. That he needed to go out first thing in the morning, but after that he was content until about 5:00 p.m.

That Weaver regretted like hell they'd never explore the sizzle and burn that arced between them.

2

───◄◆►───

Satisfaction settled over Molly as she wandered about the kitchen the next morning, making coffee and stepping behind, over and around Patch.

She sat in the breakfast nook, her coffee just a shade hotter than the dog's breath against her bare knee. Patch seemed as eager to build their relationship as she. He'd followed her around yesterday evening, slept on the floor beside her bed last night, been full of doggy smiles this morning.

"The perfect substitute," she said, stroking his black-and-white head.

The corners of his serrated lips turned down. *Back to that, are we?*

Maybe he had a right to resent his role as a replacement, but she hadn't wished for the well of emptiness in her life. In the last couple of years, though, her hormones had surged with each baby gift she'd bought. Even when she was honored as the godmother to two children and taught a roomful of bright and shiny faces every weekday from September to June.

But now she had her dog.

"Yep. Now I'm perfectly satisfied," she told Patch. "What more could a woman want?"

He whined a little, as if he didn't believe her.

Okay, okay. So she'd been thinking about Weaver Reed. Not that she wanted him or anything, *not* that, but it was an intriguing situation. A handsome hunk of single man, the guardian of a tiny baby girl.

A man looking for the fastest train out of town.

Been there, done that, she reminded herself.

So, intriguing situation or not, she was staying clear of Weaver and his baby. "I've got you," she said, sliding her hands over Patch's warm, soft fur. "What more could a woman want?"

A knowing glint entered the dog's soft brown eyes. *That's the second time you've asked me that.*

Weaver stared dully at early morning through the kitchen window as he paced by on another tour of the house. Daisy Ann rode in his arms, eyes at half-mast. He passed her room but didn't bother trying to lay her in her crib. Oh, no, he'd made that mistake already, three times during the night. The minute he set her down she started wailing, to be quieted only by endless pacing about the house. He'd never been so tired in his life.

A guy didn't go through seven foster homes between the ages of zero and eighteen without learning something about babies. He'd changed diapers, wiped runny noses, made numerous peanut butter and jelly sandwiches. But he'd never had the total care of an infant.

The nanny had established a routine he tried his best to follow. He was even pretty adept at the diapers with the tapes and could give a bath without losing his hold of slippery baby skin. But sleep. Ah, that was another matter altogether. For some reason, Daisy seemed to want to wait out the sandman from the shelter of his arms.

After three nights of this, he was approaching the fraying end of his rope. Sleep deprivation might go a long way in explaining the misunderstandings with Molly Michaels yesterday afternoon. As well as his unprecedented physical reaction to her.

But he hadn't time to think of that. He had phone calls to make, an appointment with his attorney, some sort of temporary child care to arrange for Daisy. Oh, yeah, and dishes and laundry, and if somebody didn't buy this place real soon he was going to have to take the For Sale sign off the goddamn lawn mower and put it to use.

As if she could read his frustrated thoughts, Daisy Ann started wriggling and let out a fretful cry. Weaver sighed. "It's okay, baby." He adjusted her position and patted her awkwardly on the back. "Cousin Weaver's right here."

His only happy thought was of Patch. Though he missed the dog's good-natured company, he hoped that Patch's adoption was the first event of a domino effect. The dog, the cars, the tools, the house...Daisy Ann.

That thought set her off. "You're a mind reader, lady," he said, changing her position again. She snuffled unhappily against his neck, and he picked up the pace, his mind sliding back to his yard-long To Do list.

A round of barking broke into his mulling over of item ten. Familiar barking.

Apparently challenged by the noise level, Daisy Ann upped her wailing as Weaver pulled open the front door. He groaned. Patch was back, alone.

Weaver sighed, letting the crying-barking duet wash over him. *This is the worst day of my life.*

She couldn't be more than two minutes behind Patch, Molly thought as she trotted around the corner and up the block. She'd gone out front to weed her mother's flower garden, and Patch had followed close beside her. It seemed obvious he wasn't going to run off.

Which showed you how much she knew about dogs.

She'd turned just in time to see him heading toward Weaver's, and so now she followed Patch, intent on getting him back, maybe even before the man realized she'd lost the dog.

Uh-oh. Scratch that thought. Even from the sidewalk she saw the tableau: dog, man, baby. Déjà vu.

Only different this time, she discovered as she

walked up the terra-cotta steps. Dark circles etched Weaver's eyes, and the baby who'd been sleeping yesterday was awake and cranky. Molly's heart squeezed in sympathy for them both.

Just get the dog, she admonished herself. She couldn't afford to get involved with any other temporaries.

"Come on, Patch!" she called from about ten steps away. "Sorry. Guess he just wanted to come by for a visit."

"You're not returning him?"

The relief in Weaver's voice pulled her four steps closer. She shook her head. "I just hope he's not trying to tell me something."

Weaver's smile was a pale ghost of the day before's. Her heart squeezed again.

"So this is the baby," she found herself saying as she walked even closer.

"Daisy Ann."

Daisy Ann had wide blue eyes, fat baby cheeks and blond hair like chick fuzz. Red blotches from crying mottled her skin. And it was scary as heck that Molly still thought the little girl gorgeous. She gently stroked the fretful infant's little hand. "Hi, you."

The baby hushed. Patch leaned against her leg in obvious approval.

Weaver gave another ghost smile. "Daisy Ann says hi back." He appeared to perk up a little. "Would you like to hold her?"

"No," Molly said hastily. She tried stepping away

but found Patch wedged against the back of her legs. "No, thank you." Admiring was one thing. Touching was trouble.

Weaver's wide shoulders sagged, and the baby made some mini grousing noises.

"Is she hungry?" Molly couldn't help asking. "Does she need a new diaper?"

He shook his head. "Took care of those fifteen minutes ago. She seems to be the Muhammad Ali of fighting sleep. A champion."

Molly reached down and grasped Patch's collar. "I should be going, then."

"See you around."

"Mmm." She should hope against it.

As Molly turned, a parcel service truck screeched to a halt at the bottom of the drive. A uniformed man jumped out to carry a thick manila envelope up the steps. Eyeing the burdened Weaver behind her, he shoved the package in Molly's empty hand. "Have a nice day!"

He had the truck in gear and was flying up the street before she had a chance to reply. Molly glanced at the address. "For you," she said, turning.

Weaver backed up, staring at the package as if it were a shivering mass of spiders and snakes. "For Weaver Reed?"

She checked again. "Yes."

He groaned, obviously a man in deep distress.

None of your business, Molly told herself sternly.

Asking will only involve you. She walked forward, holding out the package.

He retreated.

She frowned. "Aren't you going to take it?"

"I don't think I should be alone right now," he said, wary eyes still on the envelope. "Tell me you'll come in for coffee."

She shook her head. "I shouldn't bother you." She tightened her fingers around Patch's collar. "Take the package and we'll go."

The dog whined. Daisy Ann whined, too, sounding as though she was determined to win this round against sleep.

"You'd be doing me a favor," Weaver said.

Oh, no.

"If that envelope holds what I think it does, I could really use a shower before facing it…but I hate to put Daisy down when she's crying."

Molly should go now. Turn around before she got any nearer to the cute baby and the handsome man. She tried hardening her marshmallow heart. What did she need them for? Didn't she have her baby substitute?

"If you'd just hold her while I take a quick one, I'll make you a great cup of coffee." He grimaced. "Okay, I lied. I'll make you a passable cup of coffee."

"Well…"

Like all men, he could sniff out hesitation from a mile off. And like all men, he used a dirty trick to get what he wanted. "We'll switch. The package for her." He held out little Daisy Ann. "Just for a couple of minutes?"

Patch leaned hard against Molly and she stumbled forward. Weaver took that as eagerness, she supposed, because she found herself relieved of the parcel and with Daisy Ann in her arms. Warm and cuddly.

Molly glared at the pleased-looking Patch. "It would serve you right if I think she's better than you."

The dog sat on his wagging tail. *I'd be disappointed if you didn't.*

Molly didn't think the remark deserved a response, and as Weaver was looking at her funny, she shut her mouth and followed him into the house. Holding Daisy Ann so the baby's head rested in the shallow cup of her shoulder, Molly rhythmically patted the infant's back. Weaver showed her into the kitchen, then disappeared down a hallway.

She cradled the infant in her arms to get a better look at Daisy Ann's face. Drowsy eyes. A little smile now quirking up the corners of her baby mouth.

If admiring a baby was one thing, and touching a baby was trouble, what did that make holding one?

Desperately sweet.

Molly groaned softly. This was a really bad idea.

Weaver made the best possible use of the free minutes. He attempted sleeping and showering at the same time.

Shoulders propped against the tiled wall opposite the showerhead, he reveled in the heated spray on his chest and allowed his eyes to close.

But visions of the ominous envelope kept popping into his head. More paperwork, of course, from Baker, Baker, Baker and Kennedy, Attorneys at Law. Another sharp tooth of the legal trap in which he found himself.

He'd have to pore over this new set, as well as the legal stuff already on his desk *and* take care of Daisy Ann. *And* the laundry *and* the dishes— But he'd already made himself crazy with that list.

Though he'd made a few tentative queries about child care two days ago, he'd still been arrogant enough to suppose he could take care of Daisy Ann and everything else. Now he had to get serious.

He'd ask Molly for advice. She was a local and an elementary schoolteacher. Surely she would have a few ideas.

Dressed in his last pair of clean jeans and a T-shirt, Weaver hurried down the hall to rescue Molly. He'd taken longer cleaning up than he should have, but now he felt half-alive again. He'd make her that cup of coffee he promised and pick her brain for the best possible day-care sources.

In the kitchen doorway he paused.

The aroma of freshly brewed coffee entered his bloodstream like life-giving plasma. Daisy Ann, co-

cooned in her infant seat, snoozed away in the middle of the kitchen table. Molly sipped from a steaming mug as she slipped yesterday's dishes into the dishwasher.

The silence, the fragrance and the vision hit Weaver with the impact of a brick through a windshield.

Ask Molly to be the nanny!

No calls to make, no interviews to schedule, no wasting time. She was a teacher and obviously great with kids. If Molly would agree to be Daisy's nanny, just for a few weeks until he was cleared out of here, then he could make today's appointment with the lawyer. Have the house picked up enough for a decent showing if the realtor called. Open up the newly delivered envelope and get to work.

A perfect plan, with only a couple of glitches. Glitch one: He ran his eyes up the length of Molly's lean legs. Traced the sleek fall of her hair. A lick of heat streaked through him. If he spent day after day with her, what would happen to that fire?

You'll control it, Reed. He'd have to, because he needed someone for Daisy Ann a hell of a lot more than he needed a woman. As pleasant as he was sure it would be, a relationship with Molly would only be temporary, and Daisy Ann could be a lifetime if he didn't get something else figured out soon. Both women certainly wanted someone more interested in sticking around than he was.

Which left only glitch two: Could he get Molly to agree?

He sucked in a deep breath. "Hi there," he said, and put on a friendly smile.

She started. "H-hello." She grabbed the long hem of her ragged T-shirt and stretched it down, obviously a nervous gesture.

"You made the coffee. Thanks."

She smiled a little. "Mine's generally better than passable. Try it?"

"Sure." He crossed the kitchen floor and poured himself a cup, immediately swallowing a long drink of the stuff. "Great," he pronounced.

She smiled and pushed away from the countertop. "I'll leave, then."

"But—but—"

She paused, one dark eyebrow winging up.

"Daisy Ann—"

She swung around to look at the sleeping infant. "She's fine."

"Uh, Patch…"

At the sound of his name, the dog popped out from beneath the kitchen table and trotted over to Molly. She stroked his ears. "Ready to go."

Weaver stared at the dog. *You're not helping.* "Well then, uh…me."

That eyebrow took flight again.

"You?"

He shifted from foot to foot. What could he say to make her stick around, at least to hear him out?

A short laugh broke into his thoughts. "Babied

out?'' she asked. "Would you like a little adult conversation?''

Relief must have shown all over his face because she laughed again. "I know just how you feel. A rainy couple of days cooped up with a roomful of first-graders and I long for verbal fights over politics rather than wadded paper towels at ten paces.''

"You'll sit with me while I drink my coffee, then?'' He didn't wait for a reply but hurried to the table and pulled out two chairs. "I don't think we'll wake Daisy Ann.''

He sat and looked at Molly expectantly. With a reluctance he tried to ignore, she sat beside him. She pulled down on the front hem of her T-shirt again.

To keep things strictly professional, he trained his gaze on her face. She stuck out her lower lip as she concentrated on a small hole she'd found in the fabric about halfway down the front of the shirt.

Looking at her lips wasn't helping any.

"So, uh, you have the summer off, then?'' he asked.

She didn't look up. "Mmm-hmm.''

"I'm swamped with things to do.''

She nodded, one hand gripping the hem tauter, one finger tracing the little hole she'd found.

"That package that came today is the last straw,'' he said.

Her finger paused and her grip slackened on the shirt. "What's inside? Felt as thick as a book.''

He shook his head. "Not a book, though I feel like I could write one after the past few weeks."

"On baby care?" She smiled.

"Be serious." But he eagerly grabbed ahold of the conversation topic. "What kind of book do you think I'd write?"

"Hmm." She considered a moment, then the corners of her full lips turned up. "From the looks of your fridge, I'll have to rule out a cookbook."

He gave a laugh, then quickly stifled it when Daisy Ann twitched. "No cookbook."

Brow wrinkling, she pulled the T-shirt tight again. Weaver grimaced.

Her finger retraced the hole. "Maybe some sort of fix-it book. Or craft." She looked up. "Yes, that's it."

"Craft? What makes you say that?" Weaver brought his coffee mug to his mouth.

She tilted her head, her distinctive silvery gray eyes considering him. "You have that rugged, outdoorsy look. Like you spent summers in Maine, learning the craft of carving canoes from your father."

He nearly spit out his coffee in surprise. Instead, he coughed, then swallowed the stuff down. "Wrong. No Maine. No canoes. No dad." *Nobody.*

She pursed her lips. "No? Well, I give up. Just tell me. What do you really do?"

"I started with ten years of military service." Weaver propped his elbows on the table.

"Wait," she said, holding out her hand. "Let me guess. Marines."

He reared back. "Please. I'm retired navy, ma'am."

"Unpardonable insult?"

"Forgivable error," he corrected.

"What do you do now?"

Trace drug money. Recover stolen artifacts. Rescue kidnapped children. He shifted in his chair, uneasy with how he should answer. "I'm kind of a—of a— private spy."

"A what?" she asked mildly, obviously thinking she'd heard wrong.

"A private spy."

Her brows drew together, then eased. "Oh, come on." She laughed. "Tell me what you really do."

"Really. I work for a small private company that hires ex-military intelligence officers."

She shook her head, laughing again. "Next you're going to tell me that you're not wearing your real face." She leaned toward him. "This is just plastic, right?" She laid her fingers against his cheek.

Branded. Her hand was cool, but still he felt the touch sizzle into his skin. She immediately pulled away as if she burned, too, but he caught her fingers before they had a chance to escape him.

Against his palm they felt fragile, yet the tension running down her arm was strong. "I told you the truth," he said. "And the other truth is I hoped I could talk you into helping me."

Her fingers fluttered a little against his hand, but she didn't pull back. "Help you?"

"Yeah." He tried a friendly smile. "I was in the middle of planning a job when, uh—" he gestured at the infant seat "—enter Daisy Ann."

"This is beginning to sound vaguely familiar."

Familiar? How many nanny-needing spies had this woman met?

A disdainful expression crossed her face and she pulled her hand free. "You're a spy and you need my help, right? Pick up a briefcase and drop it someplace? But no, that isn't right."

"Of course it isn't—"

She snapped her fingers. "I've got it! You say someone's following you. We end up at your place. You have a couple of tickets to Paris, where we'll complete our mission, pretending to be husband and wife."

Weaver blinked. "That's not what I had in mind at all."

"Oh no? It's what that used car salesman had in mind in the movie *True Lies*. He used that same spy story to troll for women."

Expression still disbelieving, she slid forward in her chair, obviously preparing to leave.

Weaver gulped. "No, no. Wait a minute. I'm not trolling. I'm offering, hoping... I need a woman." He groaned, started over. "I need a *nanny*."

Shaking her head as if pitying him, she pushed up from the table. "Come on, Patch."

Before Weaver could replay the conversation and figure out where he'd gone wrong, dog and woman rushed toward the hall leading to the front door. They paused at the kitchen threshold.

"What you really need," said the long-legged woman who was departing too quickly from his life, "is some better come-on lines."

Daisy Ann woke as the front door slammed shut behind Molly. The baby started crying again, natch.

3

---><---

Weaver leaned heavily on the handlebar of the baby jogger—sort of a three-wheeled stroller with bicycle tires—as he pushed it slowly down the sidewalk. If he was tired two days ago, what did he suffer from today?

Fatigue dehydration. He could suck up sleep as a thirsty plant sucks up water.

The warm afternoon breeze ruffled the brim of Daisy's cloth hat. Fingers crossed, he leaned over and checked her face. Her eyes remained wide open, though, and absorbed by the neighborhood sights. Weren't babies supposed to nap in the afternoon?

He rounded the corner and in a front yard up ahead caught the flash of a familiar dark coat of fur. Patch. Molly's place.

He hadn't thought of her in two days.

Absolutely true, he insisted to his guffawing inner devil. Her image played with his mind in the dark well of the *night,* when he stumbled about the house, Daisy in his arms. Anyone would dream of somebody to hand the unhappy baby over to.

"Hello, Weaver."

He practically jumped out of his exhausted skin. Lost in his own musings, he'd made it to the near corner of Molly's front yard without noticing her kneeling behind the short picket fence. Lethal-looking claw in hand, she was weeding an overgrown, casual jumble of flowers that grew against waist-high white pickets.

"How are you?" she asked politely.

He noticed she avoided looking at the baby. And because she wasn't looking directly at him, either, he stared at her long, bare legs. Energy, pure, sexual energy, surged skyward from his heels. He felt a little dizzy from the rush.

His "Fine, really fine now," was lost in the excited barking of Patch, who rushed the fence to greet them.

Weaver leaned over to stroke the dog's hot fur. "You been good for Molly?" he asked the dog.

Shifting forward, she stabbed the claw into the dirt. "The best. I'm glad we found each other."

As if he understood her, the dog whirled and swiped her face with his long tongue. Weaver felt absurdly glad that she hugged the dog's neck instead of wiping dry her cheek.

Weaver grinned. "Feeling's mutual, I guess."

She looked up, smiled briefly, then hastily put her head down. "What about your other, uh, encumbrances? Any luck with those?"

Weaver frowned. "I scared off some potential home-buyers yesterday. Miss D, here, was fussy, I hadn't gotten to the dishes yet, and then when they opened the door to the master bedroom… Well, never mind.'' He brightened. ''I did sell off the weed whapper. To the disappointed real estate agent.''

Daisy Ann let out an unhappy squeal that experience told him was the precursor to a full-out wail. He rolled the jogger back and forth to soothe her. ''Daisy and I rented *True Lies* the other night.''

That got Molly looking up again. He let himself spiral down into the liquid silver of her eyes. Cool sizzle washed over him. It took a minute to notice the funny expression on her face, like maybe she was a little embarrassed.

''You aren't *really* a spy, are you?'' she asked.

''Believe it or not, I am.'' Still rolling Daisy Ann back and forth, he crossed his heart with a finger.

Molly stared at the spot. ''No kidding?''

The baby wasn't about to be satisfied by a trek then return-trek over the same sidewalk square. She wailed her disappointment.

''Gotta go,'' he said, and pushed the jogger forward. Daisy Ann quieted, but Patch started barking and followed them the length of the fence. At the edge of Molly's property, Weaver looked back. She was standing, in another one of those holey T-shirts and skin-baring shorts, watching them walk away.

Which got him thinking.

When he reached the next corner, he turned right. And then another right at the next corner.

He headed right back toward Molly. Hadn't he seen

a little softening in her eyes? Was it possible he could convince her to be the nanny after all?

This time it was Patch who barked the first greeting. Weaver smiled his best smile at Molly as he slowly walked by. "You know," he said. "I'm still looking for a woman." Wincing at his own lousy wording, he tried again. "I mean a temporary nanny for Daisy."

Her silver eyes rounded and her mouth opened, but nothing came out. She switched her gaze from his face to Daisy. Thank God the darling had the presence of mind to yawn cutely, then let her eyes drift close. *Damn*, he thought, *you're good, kid.*

Molly never got a word out, so when he passed her property and hit the corner, he made a right, and then another right. Again, he headed right back toward Molly.

This time she was waiting for him, her head already up as he came by.

"I need some order in our lives," he said. "At this rate, I'll never get back to Maryland. My partner's getting antsy, wanting to get back out in the field."

Gabe had hated postponing their assigned mission as much as he did. Though the Czech situation was currently stable, any time now XNS would have to mobilize. After all the time he'd put into the assignment, he didn't want to miss it.

Molly didn't say anything this go-round, either, but he noticed that she didn't question his reference to his work.

He made the same circle again.

As he passed this time, she strolled along her side of the fence, keeping pace with him. He noticed her sneaking peeks at Daisy, who looked like a perfectly baited trap with her cheeks flushed and her mouth open in sleep.

"Being a spy doesn't seem like a very good job for a man with a baby," Molly said.

He nodded in agreement. "Terrible job."

She let out a long whoosh of air, focusing his attention on her lips. No lipstick. Cute little bow in the top lip. Full lower one. Not too wide. As a matter of fact, kind of prim, especially without any lipstick darkening it.

"So I suppose you're looking," she said.

He watched each word leave her lips. "Mmm," he replied, not making sense of what she'd said.

"You *are* looking?" Her silver gaze cut from Daisy to his face.

He snapped to attention. "Sure, sure, have my partner working on it." They reached the edge of her yard. He hesitated before going on, but Daisy made some ominous whimpers, so he kept moving forward.

Molly and Patch met Weaver halfway on his next turn around her block. He hid his surprise by fussing over the dog, who danced happily on the end of a leather leash.

Daisy whimpered again, so he picked up the pace a bit.

Molly chewed on her lower lip as they walked

abreast, something obviously on her mind. Then, abruptly, she stopped worrying her lip. "So, you really want me to be a temporary nanny?"

Entranced by her darkened bottom lip, he grunted out an affirmation, then swiftly realized he should take advantage of her interest. He cleared his throat. "Might you—"

"And why are you having your partner doing your job search?"

"Huh?"

"You said being a spy is a terrible occupation for a man with a baby."

"You got that right." They turned the last corner and now had a straight shot at her house.

"And you said you had your partner looking."

Weaver stopped at the pickets surrounding Molly's house. "Ah." She thought he meant Gabe was helping him find a new job, not a new family. "What I meant was my partner is looking for someone else for Daisy."

Molly stared at him. Daisy started whimpering again. Weaver began to move on, but Molly put her cool hand on his arm.

Yow. Energy flooded him. Daisy whimpered a second time, and Molly's hand left his skin. She bent over the jogger and unstrapped the baby. In seconds she had Daisy Ann against her chest.

The baby snuggled against Molly, her frilly lashes reclosing over her eyes.

She protectively cupped the back of the baby's

head, an exposé of Molly Michaels in the tender gesture. "What do you mean, looking for someone for Daisy Ann?"

Weaver ignored the cold, sad trickle that ran like a tear down his spine. The baby deserved a family. She deserved the security and permanence he'd never had and couldn't offer now.

"Molly, I need to find someone else to adopt Daisy Ann. It looks like there isn't a Reed alive in the world but me, so now we're searching for some of Daisy's mother's family."

He watched Molly swallow. Her hand pushed off the baby's funky little hat. "Someone else for Daisy Ann?" she whispered again.

"From the family." Another trickle rolled down his spine. "It's the right thing to do," he said to her. Certain, *absolutely certain*, it was true.

Molly felt each of the baby's breaths. She saw Weaver's, too, each one causing his wide chest to rise and fall. *Someone else for Daisy Ann.*

Of course it was the right thing to do. And, she reminded herself, it was *none* of her business.

But the baby felt like all her midnight yearnings and Saturday-afternoon baby-shower envy rolled into one. "She seems a little damp," Molly said, not yet ready to give Daisy up. "I'll change her if you have a diaper with you."

Weaver surrendered the disposable eagerly enough

and seemed content to play with Patch while she took Daisy Ann into the house to freshen her up.

Daisy's chubby legs performed froglike jumping jacks as Molly accomplished the diaper change on a folded towel. Resnapping the little girl's pink romper, she noticed that the garment's tag was in the front. *"Men,"* she told Daisy, and chuckled. "What they don't know..."

Daisy squealed back in agreement. Molly held the baby's warmth against her chest as she slipped off the outfit. She tried ignoring the sweet sensation of baby skin against her palm. "I think he's right," she said, noticing the little girl wore one green and one red sock. "You *do* need a nanny. Or at least someone with a little fashion sense."

Daisy squealed again, and her tuft of fine hair brushed Molly's jaw. *Sweet.*

Dry, snaps in back, mismatched socks straightened, Daisy appeared infinitely content in Molly's arms. On her way back to the front door, she stopped in the kitchen for a drink of cool water.

Nanny, nanny, nanny. The funny notion ran through Molly's mind with every gulp. "No," she whispered. The baby made a halfhearted swipe at the retreating glass and found Molly's face instead. Her little hand groped Molly's nose and forehead, and she cooed as if the discovery pleased her.

Nanny, nanny, nanny.

Molly grabbed the phone off the counter and

quickly punched a number. A hoarse voice answered the call. "Cynthia?" Molly asked. "Is that you?"

"A nauseated me," her friend answered. "When they tell you morning sickness goes away after three months, they lie."

Molly smiled. "Just the person I need to talk to. Tell me I don't want a baby."

Cynthia answered automatically. "You don't want a—hey, wait a minute! What's going on?"

"I had this crazy idea I might take a nanny position. *Temporary* nanny position."

An audible release of breath came over the phone. "Scare me, why don't you. For a minute I thought there was a man in your life you'd kept secret."

Molly cocked her head to peer down the hall. Through the open front door she saw Weaver, sun making highlights in his dark hair. His white teeth flashed as he grinned at the dog. "No man," she said firmly. "But as a nauseated mother-to-be, tell me I don't want to take on this baby. She's four months old and her name is Daisy Ann. I'm holding her right now."

Cynthia's voice altered, going from hoarse to gentle. "Four months old? You're holding her right now?" She sighed. "Don't tell Carl, but I hope for a girl. All those darling pink dresses, little pink ballet slippers…"

Molly stopped listening and just stared down at Daisy's green and red socks. "You're not helping, Cynthia."

Her friend continued rattling on. "Is she just a love to hold? That's such a cute stage, and—"

"Bye, Cynth." Molly clicked off the call and, desperate now, immediately dialed another familiar number. This time a wailing baby sounded in the background. "Dana. I'm hoping against hope you'll tell me I don't want a baby."

The baby's crying cut off. "Sorry about that," Dana said. "It's bottle time. What did you say?"

"I met this man—" Molly cleared her throat and started again. "There's this baby that needs a nanny. Temporarily. I was thinking of taking the job. Tell me I shouldn't."

A long silence. "Go back to the man part."

Molly bit her lip. "The man part is inconsequential, except for the fact that he needs help with the baby."

"Where's his wife?"

"No wife. He's not even the father." Molly sighed impatiently. "Listen, it's a long story, but the bottom line is he needs help and Daisy Ann is gorgeous and—"

"I don't think you should do it."

Molly's jaw dropped. "What?"

"Didn't you ask me to talk you out of it?"

"Well, yes, but—"

"No buts. You're on vacation. Babies give you a headache."

Molly rubbed Daisy Ann's warm back. "Baby *showers* give me a headache."

"Whatever. What's this man's name?"

"Weaver. Weaver Reed." Molly bit her lip and inhaled a breath of baby scent. "Don't you think I should be the nanny? You know I'm good with babies."

"You're great with babies. What's this Weaver look like?"

Molly stroked the fringe of hair at the back of Daisy's head. "Six feet plus. Dark hair. Great body. Great smile."

"Don't do it."

"But it would only be for a few weeks. Maybe even less."

"What about saying goodbye to the baby after a few weeks? Wouldn't that be hard?"

Daisy's wisps of hair tickled Molly's knuckles. "It would be hard to say goodbye now," she whispered.

"There you go," Dana answered briskly. "All the more reason to forget this nutty nanny idea."

Molly frowned. "It's not so nutty. You know I go stir-crazy in the summer. You said yourself I'm great with babies."

In Dana's silence, Molly could picture her friend's skeptically raised brows.

Molly frowned deeper and curled her hand protectively over the baby's head. "I don't care what you say. I'm going to do it. I'm going to tell Weaver I'll be the nanny for Daisy Ann."

The silence on the other end of the phone changed. It took on a triumphant quality.

Molly squeezed shut her eyes. "Something's

wrong here. I know I called you up to talk me out of this. But I was worried you'd probably encourage me to do it."

"Fooled you." Humor laced Dana's voice.

"Yes. I'm getting it now," Molly said slowly, just beginning to see how she'd been manipulated. "When you tried to convince me not to do it, I ended up admitting how much I wanted to."

"There's a reason I majored in psychology and you didn't." Dana laughed outright. "I'm good at it and you're not."

Weaver let the sun soak into his skin as he sat on Molly's porch steps. So tired... His eyelids drifted closed, and he heard Patch grunt as the dog settled down beside him.

Nice of Molly to change the baby. Nice Molly. He grinned a little to himself. Good to get his mind back on track. If he had a prayer of her agreeing to be the nanny, he had to think about her professionally, not pruriently. He grinned again. *Hey, I wasn't aware I even knew that word.* Maybe having a teacher around was a good influence on him.

Pattering of footsteps. A tiny *aa-hem*. In the interest of keeping his thoughts professional, Weaver kept shut his eyes.

She *aa-hemmed* again. "You asleep?" she whispered.

Oh, he wanted to be. Oh, he wanted to be sleeping in cool sheets and then wake up and look into her cool silver eyes. Wake up and warm her gaze with soft caresses, with the brush of his tongue against her shoulder—

Eyes closed was not working.

He lifted his lashes. "I'm awake." Molly stepped over Patch and then clattered down the porch steps to face him. With Daisy snuggled in her embrace, she looked at him apprehensively, two spots of color on her cheeks.

"What's up?" he asked.

Still, she hesitated.

He straightened. "Daisy doesn't have a diaper rash, does she? The nanny left this goopy stuff, but I think Daisy doesn't like being buttered up, and it gets under my fingernails and—"

"No diaper rash." Molly bit her lip. "But you had her clothes on backward."

Weaver shrugged. "I'm not too familiar with baby female clothing."

She smiled a little. "Ah, I see. Make it grown-up female clothing and you'd be an expert."

He refused to grin back. He refused to think about him pulling off Molly's T-shirt. Of him unsnapping her bra with a flick of his fingers. Of her breasts swinging toward him— He groaned.

Her smile faded. "What's the matter. Do you feel okay?"

"No," he said. "I'm dizzy."

After another minute's silence, her two front teeth clamped down on her lower lip again.

She had something to tell him, obviously something she was unsure about. "What's the matter?" he asked.

She rubbed Daisy's back. She shifted from foot to foot, then scratched one of her long, runner's calves with the toe of the other sneaker.

"Baby's asleep," he said, noticing the infant's head had fallen onto Molly's shoulder.

"Oh. Oh." She seemed pleased at the interruption and walked toward the baby jogger. In slow motion, an obvious attempt to leave Daisy undisturbed, Molly bent over and lightly deposited the baby in the seat.

Stop looking. He didn't, of course. He let his gaze freely roam those turn-on legs, slender hips, the long, fragile curve of her back. But he also noticed the gentle way her hands draped the blanket over Daisy, and noticed the attention Molly paid to adjusting the sunshade so the baby was protected.

She turned back around and crossed her arms over her chest. "I was thinking...maybe I could be Daisy's nanny."

Weaver's heart leapt, like Michael Jordan on his way up for a slam dunk. He swallowed it back down. "You will?" *Steady, boy.*

"If you want me." She looked toward Daisy Ann, a gentle smile breaking over her face. "If you think she'll like me."

"Want you? Like you?" Weaver rose to his feet and took a couple of steps toward Molly. "I could kiss you!"

Obviously alarmed, she tried to move back but was blocked by the oversize front wheel of the baby jogger.

"On the cheek," he said with mock affront.

Her smile turned embarrassed, and she shuffled forward, tilting her cheek toward him and holding out her hand.

Weaver wanted to laugh at the gesture. Covering all the bases, that was Molly. Holding out for a handshake, yet submitting to his playful bid for a kiss.

Just a firm grip and a quick buss, Reed.

Her hand disappeared in his. The fine skin of her cheek made him cross-eyed as he moved closer.

A knee-high doggy force nudged him firmly. Pushed him forward. Molly's surprised gaze swung toward his, bringing her lips his way. He and Molly made contact. Bumped each other. Lip to lip.

4

Mouth to mouth. A real kiss. The action so startled Molly that she froze.

Weaver didn't move away, either, and their lips stayed pressed together, stayed warm against warm. Molly felt the tiny bristle of whiskers at the edge of his mouth—an image of him shaving, shirtless, flicked through her mind—and then he tilted his head, pressed deeper.

Me! Me! Me! Nerve endings clamored for attention like first-graders on a Monday morning. She felt the brush of his tongue on her bottom lip, the sensation of his breath on the skin of her cheek. Her heart pounded the beat of passion—*boom, boom, boom.*

Must've been the wakeup call, because suddenly Weaver jerked back. He straightened and stared down at her, his breath labored.

His hands dived deep into his pockets. "When can you start?" A pained expression scrunched his brow, and he cleared his throat.

Weaver held his breath. Damn that accidental lip-lock. She wouldn't cancel her offer because of his purposeful deepening of the kiss, would she? He hoped she'd go along and just pretend it never happened, because he couldn't think of another way to deal with the thing.

"Tomorrow," she said.

He tried not to stare at the shape of her mouth. Tried forgetting the smooth texture, the sweet taste.

"I'll start tomorrow morning." Her gaze left his face, and she turned her head to look at the snoozing Daisy.

Weaver released an inward sigh. Ignoring the arrival of the Fourth of July on a June afternoon seemed to work for Molly, too. He grasped the handle of the baby jogger and turned it toward the sidewalk. Yeah, she wanted to pretend the fireworks hadn't happened, he thought.

Unless she hadn't felt them.

His male ego did a quick double take. *Nah.* Just one look at her flushed cheeks and her darkened lips told him that the sparks had showered Molly, too.

That didn't mean he shouldn't forget about the whole thing, though. He should forget it.

Would forget it.

Nah.

As she walked to Weaver's the next morning, Molly mentally adjusted her imaginary uniform. It was nurse's whites or a nun's habit or something, *anything*, that would keep her perspective on the job.

She had agreed to be a temporary nanny. That meant providing care. Not *caring*.

That sweet little girl wasn't hers, and the man, well, the man had nothing to do with the job at all!

The accidental kiss and her heated response to it were warnings that she intended to listen to. Don't get involved. Take care of the baby. Ignore the man.

But of course he opened the door, and she couldn't check her immediate leap of interest. She ran her gaze from his bare feet, up legs in threadbare blue jeans, to his T-shirt stretched across his chest, on to his stubbled chin, his sexy mouth, his feverish eyes—

Feverish eyes? "What's the matter, Weaver?" Two spots of color dotted his cheeks, and his eyes were heavy but overbright. "Are you sick?"

He blinked at her, slow. "I can't be sick," he said stubbornly. "I don't have time to be sick."

Patch surged forward on the leash in her hand and licked Weaver's fingers. "You're certainly not well," Molly said.

He took two steps back and slid down onto the bench in the entryway, as if he couldn't stand any longer. "I'm just tired." The back of his head bumped the wall with an audible *thunk*. "Is it tomorrow already?" The question seemed to make perfect sense to him.

"It's tomorrow and I've come to take care of Daisy Ann," she said briskly, reminding herself of her job and her one and only charge. "Where is she?"

"Just had a bottle and is napping in her crib."

"Go to bed, then," Molly said, unhooking the leash from Patch's collar. "I'm here now."

He tilted his head. "You're here now. That's nice." He stood up, weaved a little.

Molly grasped her hands behind her back to keep from reaching out to him.

He turned to walk down the hall toward what must be the bedrooms, keeping one hand against the wall. "You're here. Nice. Nice. I'm going to bed now."

"Take some aspirin," she called out. "I'll bring you some lunch later."

"Don't have to do that," he mumbled.

She sighed. "I know."

"You're here for Daisy."

She sighed again. "I promise to remember that."

The last door on the right shut behind Weaver, and Molly started her new job—her *temporary nanny* job—by familiarizing herself with the house.

Patch stuck close to her side, his warmth against her legs reassuring. The house was older, like her parents' house, with hardwood floors and real plaster walls that echoed the dog's clicking toenails. A large living room, formal dining room, white-tiled kitchen and a family room occupied the front portion of the home. Molly ventured down the long hallway only far enough to peek in the first bedroom, where she found Daisy sleeping in her crib.

She exchanged a warning look with Patch, and then they quietly walked from the bedroom back to the kitchen. Molly surveyed the cluttered counter space.

"He's not much of a housekeeper, huh?" she asked the dog.

Patch let out a big yawn agreement, then flopped to the floor.

Pots and pans, albeit clean, were stacked on top of the stove. Bottles and cans of formula occupied an entire countertop. On the opposite counter sat the microwave, door open. Inside was a scorched box of congealed...

"French toast?" Molly guessed, peering at the contents. "Pancakes?" She looked at the untouched breakfast then back toward Patch speculatively.

Don't even think about it. The dog's aversion to the leftovers was written across his face. *Unless it includes sausage.*

Molly sighed and tossed the box in the garbage. "Wonder if he had dinner last night—" She broke off the thought, trying to break off her concern, as well. *Just Daisy Ann.* Hadn't she become overinvolved with a temporary man before?

She busied herself tidying up. A couple of layers down she located instructions for Daisy's bottle preparation and a feeding schedule, both written in Weaver's bold, slashing handwriting—she recognized it from the Everything Must Go! flyer.

Then Daisy cried. Both Molly and Patch scurried down the hall before the sound might disturb Weaver. The baby blinked at Molly as she lifted the warm weight into her arms, but settled against her naturally enough, after one or two more small whimpers.

Molly turned away from the crib to run—*smack*—into a wide, bare chest.

Weaver stared down at her, apparently undisturbed by the fact that he was entirely naked except for a pair of silky boxers. "Oh. Yeah," he said, as if just remembering who she was and why she was there.

His hair was mussed, and if possible, the shadow on his jaw had darkened in the last hour. "Yeah," she echoed. His blue boxers had a humorous saying squiggled in white all over them. Sunday. Monday. Any Day. Any Way. Molly didn't think it was all that funny.

Daisy chortled, though, craning her neck to look at Weaver. To give herself some breathing room, Molly placed her palm against his solid chest and pushed. He didn't budge, so she said the first thing that came into her head. Her concern for him, naturally. "You're so hot."

"I think that's the nicest thing you've ever said to me." The words sounded hoarse, and even though he battled a fever, his half grin managed to crimp her insides.

She pushed against his disturbing heat again. "Move. You're breathing germs all over Daisy and me."

He quickly stepped back, then weaved on his feet, the way he'd done when she'd arrived. One arm still holding the baby, Molly wrapped her other hand around his massive forearm. Her fingers dug into the hard sinews to steady him.

"Ouch," he said.

Molly quickly removed her hand.

He half smiled again, then moved back a few steps so he could lean against the doorjamb. "Finding everything you need?"

She wanted him to go back to his bedroom. She needed him to go away so she could concentrate on being the impersonal, competent nanny. Daisy squirmed in her arms, and Molly automatically turned her, facing her toward Weaver. The baby wriggled again and let out a frustrated squeal.

Weaver made a funny face at the baby, lifting his eyebrows in a Groucho leer while crossing his eyes. Daisy stilled, then smiled and squealed again, a delighted squeal.

A huge chunk of Molly's resolve crumbled away. He made another silly face, and Molly made herself look over his shoulder instead, shoring up her weakening good intentions by reminding herself what she was here for.

And what she wasn't here for.

The temporary nanny wasn't here to drool over the temporary man.

Daisy crowed again with delight.

"I don't see how you'll be able to leave her." Without volition, she said the thing that bothered her most.

He stilled, and his gaze cut toward her. "I'll make sure she'll be happy. I'll find someone related to her."

"But not you."

He shrugged. "I'm no family man."

She'd heard that one before. And learned that when a man said he didn't want a baby and a home that she should listen.

So she shouldn't be interested in Weaver. She shouldn't want to take his temperature, or serve him chicken soup, or bathe his fevered brow. She certainly shouldn't want to kiss him.

And as if he sensed her disapproval, he abruptly straightened and headed through the doorway. "Call me if you need me," he said.

He didn't even linger long enough to hear her whispered, "I won't."

Daisy Ann fell asleep after her lunchtime bottle. Hoping to throw a load of Daisy's things in the washer, Molly resisted an urge to cuddle the sleeping baby and put her down in her crib instead. As she turned to tiptoe out, an open chest in the corner of the room caught her eye.

Molly knelt before it. Smelling of cedar, it was a typical hope chest, intended for the keepsakes of a bride. As she peered inside, Molly's eyes pricked with hot tears.

There were keepsakes inside, all right. Personal things, all the things Molly suddenly realized were missing from the comfortably furnished house, were placed carefully inside the chest. Framed wedding photographs of Daisy's mother and father. A picture of newborn Daisy. A wedding veil wrapped in tissue, a pink bubble-gum cigar, one of many that Molly imagined Daisy's dad had proudly passed around.

Little and big mementos to link Daisy Ann to the parents she would never know.

Molly hunched her shoulder to dry her wet cheek against her T-shirt. Every item touched her, wrenched her heart, squeezed out tears. But as moving as the keepsakes themselves was the knowledge of the one who had so carefully saved them. Not some friend of Daisy's parents, not the previous nanny.

No, each item was meticulously labeled in the distinctive handwriting she already recognized. Mr. Temporary, Mr. I'm-No-Family-Man, had taken the time and trouble to select the family memories that Daisy would take to her new life.

Weaver came awake in early morning's dim light. He stretched beneath the twisted bedclothes, realizing he didn't ache, didn't burn, didn't feel any leftovers of the illness except a sticky saltiness to his skin.

A brief warm shower in the bathroom next to his room took care of that problem. Now even more alert, he padded down the hall to Daisy's room. She slept soundly under a neatly folded baby blanket. Obviously Molly had taken good care of her the day before.

Back in the hallway, Weaver noted a dull glimmer of light shining beneath the fourth bedroom door. Frowning, he strode the few steps and palmed open the door, swinging it inward silently. The room functioned as an office, and light from a small banker's lamp spilled over the desk and onto the nearby leather couch.

Spilled like a moonbeam onto Molly's tousled hair.

Weaver sucked in air. The nanny slept as soundly as her charge, curled on her side beneath a crocheted afghan. Suddenly he remembered Molly coming to his room last night, bringing a dinner tray and then bullying him into eating the soup and crackers. She'd touched his cheek and forehead with her palm, all the while grumbling something about hope and his chest.

A feverish tremor ran through him, and he wished he could blame it on the flu. Instead he knew it was a reaction to Molly.

He commanded his feet to back off, back away, but his size twelves stepped forward and he found himself settling into the stiff-backed chair beside the desk.

He liked listening to her breathe.

He stared at the sweet curve of her cheek, the promising roundness of her body beneath the afghan she'd pulled around herself. He remembered again the tender touch of her hand against his skin.

As if she heard his presence, her eyes opened. She blinked a couple of times then smiled at him sleepily. "Are you okay?" Her voice sounded hoarse. Sexy. "Do you need something?"

"I'm fine," he said. "All better."

"And Daisy?"

He had to smile back. "In dreamland."

She untucked her hands from beneath her cheek to

reveal a stuffed elephant made of soft terry. "Pillow," she explained, stretching. Then she sat up slowly.

The elephant had creased her cheek. The afghan slid off her shoulders, revealing the T-shirt he remembered her wearing the day before. His gaze fell to the floor beside the couch and onto her jean shorts, just a scrunched puddle of denim beside her scuffed running shoes.

He liked the elephant mark on her cheek, her warm smile, the fact that she'd stayed the night when he and Daisy needed her.

A weird longing knocked on his doorless heart.

That's it. He slapped his hands on his thighs. *Time to go.* Feeling warm and fuzzy toward the nanny was a bad idea.

"I'm hungry," he said, though he didn't want food. He needed to get away, and the kitchen seemed a logical escape.

Her arms stretched toward the ceiling. "Me, too. I'll make waffles if you fry the bacon."

What could he say? Next thing he knew he was dodging bacon splatters and Patch's tail while Molly one-handedly whipped up buttermilk batter. With her free arm, she balanced Daisy on one hip.

The food tasted delicious. Thank God Molly read the newspaper in the same sequence he did. Without their unashamed squabble over who got the sport section first—followed by a ten-dollar bet on the baseball standings by the All-Star break—the morning hours might have been too comfortable.

Dishes went to the person least suited to put Daisy down for her morning nap.

"I hate the smell of dish-washing liquid," he grumbled.

"How do you feel about a dirty diaper?" Molly sent a significant look in Daisy's direction.

He simply changed his story. "I love the smell of dish-washing liquid," he answered, grabbing dishes and dashing for the kitchen sink.

Kitchen chores accomplished, he headed for the stack of paperwork in the office. He found Molly, her hair smoothly brushed and rebraided, sitting on the couch again. For some reason, he dropped back into the straight chair and watched her tie her shoelaces then neatly fold the afghan.

She laid the blanket on her lap and gazed about the room. "It's cozy in here," she said. "The whole house is cozy."

Cozy.

The word startled Weaver like the chu-chunk of a loading shotgun. He must be going soft! Inhaled too much baby powder or something. Here he was, sharing another cozy moment with a cozy woman in a cozy house.

God.

He had no business sharing cozy. He had no business looking at Molly like he had, and she had no business looking at him like she was right now. As if he were husband and daddy material, or date bait at the very least.

His mind said run, but for some crazy reason his feet stayed firmly fixed to the floor.

He swallowed, thinking fast. "It's sure nothing like my town house in Maryland. I bought it furnished and decorated—in bachelor drab—from another guy in the company." *There.* He crossed his arms over his chest. Surely she'd get his meaning.

"Oh, this house must be a welcome change, then."

She didn't get it.

Weaver tried again. With words, that is, because his body still failed to respond to his command to leave the room. "My place doesn't bother me. I'm hardly ever there."

"You don't live with anybody?"

Ah. Now they were getting somewhere. "Nope. I like living alone. I like being alone."

She nodded, as if the picture was coming into focus. "There's not a woman in your life, then?"

He leaned forward—his body seemed willing enough to move *toward* Molly—and rested his elbows on his knees. "Not permanently. Never permanently. Never *cozily.*"

Molly laughed.

Startled, Weaver straightened.

"I get it," she said, and chuckled again.

He blinked. "Get what?"

"What you're trying to tell me. You were worried that I was getting a little too comfortable here."

He shifted uneasily in his chair. "I don't know what you mean."

She laughed again. "Give it up, Reed. You thought maybe I was taking this playing house too seriously."

He wiped his palms against his pant legs. "I did not."

She shook her head. "You don't need to worry. I can recognize your type from a hundred yards and I'm immune to 'em."

"What's that supposed to mean?" He didn't like being a "type."

"You're a temporary. Temporarily in one place. Temporarily interested. Temporarily interesting. And I have a pearl-encrusted wedding gown, three moderately pukey bridesmaids' dresses and enough engraved and unused wedding invitations to keep me innoculated for the rest of my life."

The "temporarily interesting" kind of hurt. "And how do you know so much about it?" He frowned. "And where does a crusty wedding dress fit into the picture?"

She rolled her eyes. "*Pearl-encrusted.* I made the mistake of thinking I might marry a temporary once upon a time."

"Why'd you do that?"

She shrugged and looked away. "Just one of those ten stupid things that women do. He thought I could change him. I thought I could change him. That our love would change him."

Weaver already hated the guy. "You're lucky to be rid of him."

"That's right," she said. "I want marriage and family. So now I don't let your type get to me. I'm not inclined or interested, and I'm unable to fool myself."

"Fool yourself?"

"That I could ever change a man. She crossed her arms over her chest. "That a man *can* ever change. You're either born with the love-and-family gene or you're not."

"I'll give you that," he said. The one thing in his background he was sure about was that the Reeds lacked the "family" strand of DNA. He scooted forward on the seat of the chair and leaned toward Molly. "However, I'd like to voice an objection to 'temporarily interesting.'"

She sat up straight, pressing back into the leather sofa. "That's your ego talking." The banker's lamp, still on, spotlighted a fluttering pulse in her throat.

Probably. But it seemed that his ego had more to say. "And maybe I don't believe you're immune, either." Scooting farther forward until his knees bumped hers, he put his hands on the couch on either side of her thighs.

"Well, I am," she said staunchly, though the telltale pulse kicked up.

"You know as well as I do that there's some sort of attraction between us."

She didn't meet his eyes. "It means nothing."

"So if I kissed you, you'd feel nothing."

She nodded. "Right." Her voice was almost a whisper.

"Just like the other day."

Her eyes widened a tiny bit, and satisfaction drove through him. "What about the other day?" she said.

Nice try. "When we shared that kiss by mistake."

She half smiled nervously. "Oh. *That.* You said it. A mistake."

His thumbs inched over and stroked her thighs, making contact with the warm skin between her shorts and her knees.

She jumped as he found her smooth flesh. "A mistake," she said again.

"Wanna bet? Another ten bucks?"

She squared her shoulders. "Fine," she said. "Not money, though. Dishes for a week."

But he wasn't listening. Because the closer he got to her mouth, the less he heard from his ego and the more something...*else* was taking over. He'd call it sex, lust, libido, because it heated his blood, but it was twisted up with a tender emotion that...

His train of rational thought derailed.

5

Go ahead and kiss me, Molly thought. *I'll prove to you I am immune.*

His mouth descended, hot and hard.

Heat blossomed on her skin and the strand of his hair that fell against her brow did nothing to cool her.

Oh, he tasted good. Toothpaste. Ninety-nine and forty-four hundredths percent pure soap. She parted her lips to inhale his warm breath, and he slid his tongue across the inner surface of her lower lip. She trembled.

Dishes were hers this week, she thought dazedly.

With a last effort, her fingers dug into the afghan on her lap, then surrendered to travel up the rigid columns of his arms. Her hands curled around his biceps. He slanted his mouth, pushing her willing lips open for his tongue.

Sweet invasion. He connected with her, his tongue running against her teeth, the roof of her mouth, rubbing against her own tongue as if he needed to know every surface. A moan. Hers. He groaned in response.

Maybe she tugged, maybe he fell forward. Whichever it was, suddenly he was on the couch beside her. Her arms circled his neck and he groaned again, his mouth pressing harder.

Heck, this felt so right. Lying against his torso, she shifted her legs restlessly, trying to untangle them from the blanket, which had unfolded and was strangling them.

"Molly," he said against her mouth.

"That's me," she answered around the kiss, still struggling with the afghan.

He was sitting on a twist of blanket, and he rolled on one hip to jerk it free. Released, the afghan slid to the floor, revealing her bare legs, her shorts, the hem of her old T-shirt riding up around her midriff.

No time to sense the cool wash of air. From ankle to thigh, Weaver's big hand stroked a hot path. "Honey."

No time to question anything, not when his lips fell onto hers again, not when his tongue thrust its way to the hot heart of her mouth. His palm slid to her other thigh, traveled over her shorts, skimmed the clenching muscles in her belly.

Her heart booming, she tangled her tongue with his. This feels so right.

The maddening man lifted his head. "Honey?" His voice was deep and hoarse. "You make me crazy."

Crazy. The word braked her heart to a shuddering stop. That's right. This was crazy. The whole idea of necking with Weaver was nuts. Certifiable.

"We have no reason to be kissing," she said. They

had no future, and she was years past kissing for the fun of it. She ran a hand over her face, keenly aware of each of his five fingers spread across her midriff.

"Then we'll stop," he said, resolve just as thready in his voice. But his hand merely flexed against her skin.

Beneath her bra, her nipples tingled. "Okay." Molly ignored the sensation and closed her eyes, bracing for the absence of his touch.

His hand didn't move. "Maybe I can give you a reason."

She opened her eyes to see in his not humor but need.

"I'll be generous here. We can make that bet double or nothing."

The pure ridiculousness of the offer made Molly laugh, then made her want to kiss him again.

He must have seen it on her face, because his lips came down satisfyingly hard. She pressed her tongue forward, entered his mouth, heard him groan. *Oh, I've been waiting for this my whole life,* Molly thought.

Lifetimes later, he lifted his head to pull in a ragged breath.

"Weaver," she whispered, just to hear herself say his name. The sound of want in her voice made her tremble more, and his hand flexed again on her midriff.

He stared at her and put on a halfhearted grin. "Want another kiss? Could be fun."

Cold reason doused her. Fun. *She* wanted more.

She'd always wanted it all. The man, the house, the baby. This felt so right, but...

"No," she said.

Molly heard crying. For a tiny second she thought it might be her heart, then realized Daisy Ann had awakened. Daisy Ann, her temporary charge, the temporary baby of this temporary man.

Weaver heard it, too. He straightened, his hand leaving Molly's skin to automatically smooth down her T-shirt. They both rose from the couch.

He cradled her cheek in his wide, masculine palm. "You're sure?" he asked.

His eyes betrayed no feeling, his expression remained blank. Against her ribs, Molly's heart slammed. It felt too big, too fragile.

She nodded. "Dishpan hands can be terminal."

A wave of something—pain? regret?—crossed his face. "Yeah," he said. "You're right."

"Wrong again," Gabe told Weaver over the phone. "I have not been using up my sick days *or* my vacation."

"Then how come you haven't found a soul to take Daisy Ann?" Weaver heard the racking frustration in his voice.

"What's the matter, big guy. Tired of changing diapers and warming bottles?"

"I have a nanny now," Weaver muttered.

"So what's your problem?"

Weaver muttered again. "The nanny's my problem." *Big problem.*

Two days ago Daisy had come down with the same flu that had flattened Weaver. Though the pediatrician declared the bug nothing serious, thankfully Molly had moved into the house to provide Daisy Ann with round-the-clock care. And provide Weaver with round-the-clock frustration.

"Not exactly Mary Poppins, huh?"

Weaver closed his eyes. God, if only Molly would wear a pin-striped blouse and a long skirt. Hold an umbrella over her pretty face. Instead, her fresh smile and her daily getup of T-shirt and shorts were driving him to the edge.

That and the two of them on the office couch. He'd yet to find a way of dealing with the memory.

"Not exactly Mary Poppins," he confirmed.

"Any bites on the house?"

Weaver sighed. "Don't bring that up. If someone doesn't offer soon, I'm gonna have to cut the front lawn."

"Better do it today. You need to go for that curbside appeal."

"What the hell is curbside appeal?"

"Saw it on one of those cable TV home shows," Gabe answered. "You have something like seven seconds to attract a buyer. They drive past and make up their minds if they're interested almost immediately. Maybe it's three seconds."

"Seven seconds?" Weaver repeated stupidly.

"*Three* seconds?" Hell. He was in big trouble. The front yard was looking more ragged by the day, and a quick sell was his only path to sanity. He needed to get back to his old life.

He needed to get away from Molly.

He needed to find that family for Daisy Ann.

Which brought him back to Gabe. "Tell me you're doing everything to find someone for Daisy."

His partner's voice lost its normally lighthearted edge. "You know I am. I want the best for her, too." He cleared his throat. "Don't worry about things here at my end. Worry about the house and that nanny."

Weaver groaned. "Don't get me thinking about the nanny." He desperately cast about for a distraction. "The house. Now *that* I can do something about."

Weaver did what he could. He washed the front windows until they sparkled, realizing it wasn't so different from washing dishes—something every foster kid learned early. The front flower beds got weeded—another piece of cake. To reward his domesticity he allowed himself to wash the two cars he was selling. Washing and waxing the sedans wasn't really necessary, but at least it was a familiar task. Detailing cars was a guy thing, not just a *suburban* guy thing.

Finally, only one task remained. The overgrown lawn. At the far corner of the front yard, Weaver stared down the lawn mower. The thing loomed large and ferocious and he wondered if he'd need a whip and chair to tame it.

"Mind control won't work," said an amused, feminine voice. "You have to pull the cord and then push the thing."

Weaver refused to even glance Molly's way. He already knew how she looked—effortlessly appealing in running shorts and a man-size T-shirt. Hair in a braid, yards and yards of leg.

"I think I can mow the lawn without your help." He knew he sounded grumpy, but hell, she *made* him grumpy. Those legs. The silver eyes. The memory of her sweet kisses. All three tangling with her unabashed love for Patch and her tender warmth toward Daisy. *Groan.*

"Okay." But she sat down on the porch steps, stretching out her legs in front of her, gripping the baby monitor tightly. If the baby made a peep, the sound would come through the wireless transmitter loud and clear. "Daisy's feeling better, I think. She looks snuggled in for a long nap."

A spurt of relief diluted Weaver's rotten mood. Daisy on the mend. Good. Now just to get this place spiffed up and off his hands. With a deep breath, he pulled the lawn mower's cord.

Nothing happened.

With gritted teeth, he pulled again.

Sputter and die.

Pull.

Sputter and die again.

Over the outdoor smells, Molly's tantalizing scent floated by his nose. He didn't turn around. Hell, any guy should be able to operate a lawn mower. He gave it another pull. Quasi sputter.

"Need some help?"

As he suspected, she'd come up behind him. "I think I can get it," he grumbled.

"Ever operate a lawn mower?"

"Sure," he bluffed. *Like I ever wanted to.*

"Sure?"

He turned, ignoring the laughter glinting in her eyes. "Okay, I lied. See, there's a reason I'm not cut out for this 'burbs life-style. No lawn mower license."

Her laugh bubbled out. "No need to get defensive. But here's a hint—a lawn mower like this one is kinda like a car."

He stared down at the stubborn beast. "A car?" It looked nothing like the sleek and reasonable Porsche in his garage in Maryland.

Molly had a seriously sexy little dimple in her cheek that he'd never noticed before. It showed up now, all flirty, kicking up his heartbeat and tickling his libido. "Runs on gas," she said, nodding to the mower. "And I think this baby's out."

Double groan.

His plans for the yard proceeded more smoothly after that. Molly returned to the house. He located a gas can in the backyard shed and after another couple of tries got the mower humming.

He'd never noticed the smell of cut grass before. In the lazy June sunshine it smelled...good...pungent and satisfying. The rows he mowed into the overgrown grass were even and smooth. *I can do this*, he thought smugly. He could see the headlines now: Man From Concrete Childhood Conquers Southern California Suburbia.

Still feeling like a warrior, he rolled the lawn mower back to the driveway. It wheeled easily into its place in the row of yard-care items he wanted to get rid of. Bending over to grab the For Sale sign off the drive, Weaver caught another whiff of the gasoline-and-grass-cuttings blend. The smell of success. He chuckled to himself and moved to hang the hand-lettered cardboard from the mower's throttle.

The sign wouldn't hang correctly. In response to his minute adjustments, it slid way right, then left. Finally at an even dangle, a spurt of breeze flipped it over wrong side out.

Weaver threw the frustrating sign away. He'd make another, bigger one. Later.

He turned back to the lawn, satisfaction rising higher as a butterfly cartwheeled across the newly clipped grass. Yeah, he'd conquered suburbia. Surely he could conquer his other problems, too.

Family for Daisy Ann and—

"Look what I found!" Molly's butterfly-bright voice came from behind him.

Weaver closed his eyes. And certainly he could squash his attraction to her. He swung around slowly.

Baby monitor clipped to her waistband, Molly walked to him, one hand balancing a short stack of fence boards on her shoulder, the other holding a lethal-looking power tool.

Damn her. She stood there, sunlight sparking highlights in her dark hair, her silver eyes gleaming like moonlight. Heat and cold. Baked Alaska again. A woman shouldn't get to him like this.

"Daisy woke for her bottle and is back to sleep again," Molly said. "And I found these at the side of the house." She waved the tool in the direction of the boards. "The backyard fence could use some repairs. I thought maybe we could do them together."

Together? Doing anything with Molly had been cut from his agenda two mornings before. "I'll take care of it myself," he said, making a grab for the boards.

She held on to them. "I can help."

He pulled harder. "Let me." He said it nicely, through gritted teeth, then with a tug slid the boards from her grasp. Assuming the weapon in her right hand had some fence-mending purpose, he grabbed that, as well. Though carefully, to avoid the slightest brush of her fingers.

Avoiding her meant avoiding any touch of her, too.

"It's a cordless drill," she said. "Be careful."

Glad the weapon was IDed, Weaver hefted its unfamiliar weight in his hand. "Used one a thousand times."

"Guess it comes in handy on those spy jobs."

He skirted her and the smile in her eyes. "Right,"

he said, moving in the direction of the broken fence and some much needed solitude.

Solitude that lasted about ninety-seven seconds.

She appeared in his peripheral vision, Patch at her side, just as he aimed the drill in the direction of a screw holding up a half-broken fence board. Thanks to the silky swing of her braid from back to breast, the drill's point rumbled and bumped aimlessly, about two inches from its intended target.

"Used one a thousand times?" Her brows rose in false innocence.

"Yeah," he said testily, pulling his gaze away from her. This time, she carried a can of paint and some other gear. "It's why they recruited me at XNS. My ability with power tools." With slightly more deftness, he removed the offending screw and ripped away the rotting board from the fence railing.

She silently handed him a new board and a couple of screws from a jar she'd also carried out.

Two more screws went into her mouth, then she knelt to position the fence board against the lower railing.

He stared down at her bent head. If only she'd go back to the house. Just her presence—the shining darkness of her hair, her light scent—was getting under his skin. Making him...itchy again.

"Gbo ahib." The screws between her lips wiggled when she talked.

He translated the comment as "Go ahead," and momentarily resigned, he pulled the weapon's—

drill's—trigger to screw the board to the higher fence rail. As he leaned into the task, his knee brushed the lean warmth of her shoulder. Sparks of awareness shot up his leg. He set his teeth and closed his eyes against the pleasure.

Wha-u-u-u.

Whining drill signaled he'd overdone the job. He jerked his knee, then the drill, away.

"Ow dith u behum a spy, anyay?" he heard her ask around the screws.

How did I become a spy, anyway? He looked down at her, grimaced. "You're not buying power-drill prowess, huh?" Restless, he shifted his feet, and his knee brushed her again. This time, she edged away.

"I..." Weaver frowned. "I was recruited. By one of my retired COs—commanding officers—in the navy." Captain Benson now ran a smaller, domestic-jobs-only firm in Southern California.

She momentarily pulled the screws out of her mouth. "That explains how. But why'd you say yes?"

"Why?" He hesitated.

Her silver-clear eyes turned upward, toward him.

He found himself talking. "Because...I was trained for it. Because I like the excitement and adventure. Because it was something a guy like me can do."

She seemed satisfied. He screwed in the second top screw. Knelt beside her to work on the bottom ones. As she held the board straight, for expediency's sake, he even used his fingers to pop the two screws she was holding out of her mouth. He didn't for a moment dwell on the shape of her lips or how they had tasted.

Like hell. He dwelled, but then forced his attention back to the fence. The quicker he got it done, the quicker he could escape from her disturbing presence.

Together, they replaced five more broken fence boards. Task completed, they both stepped back to inspect the repairs. Her shoulder bumped gently against his bicep, a companionable, couple-y touch.

And instead of alarm, he felt a satisfying buzz, not unlike the warm hum of the drill in his palm. In the face of a job well-done, his mood lightened again, and he grinned. "Aren't power tools great?"

She grinned back. "Move over, Tim Allen."

His smile faded. "Who's that? An old boyfriend?"

She laughed. "No, the star of a sitcom about a tool-toting proverbial suburban husband and father."

Suburban husband and father? "I'm nothing like that guy."

She shrugged and walked toward the paint can and the brushes.

"I'm not," he said, following her. "I told you, I like excitement, adventure."

She stirred the paint with a stick she found on the ground. "You said you had a job a guy like you can do."

"Exactly right." He nodded and picked up one of the brushes.

"So what does that mean—a guy like you?" She

dipped her brush in the can and stroked it against one of the brand-new boards.

He hated the way it reminded him of her fingertips moving against his chest. And that reminded him of the intimacy of finding her in the morning dimness, of watching her sleep within that circle of light on the couch. And then, crazy as it sounded, it was just a half step to another, almost deeper kind of intimacy—working on a home together while the sun beat down and the bees droned and the baby slept inside.

"A guy like you. What did you mean by that?" she asked again.

He tightened his hold on his paintbrush and moved toward the can. "A guy like me." Wasn't it obvious? "A guy with no need for family, no need for responsibilities."

Their knuckles bumped as they both dipped into the can at once. Fingernail tracks of hot reaction to the touch tickled up his arm.

Their gazes met. He waded hip-deep into cool silver.

Damn. He just had to face it. There was no way he could avoid his attraction to her. Even if he hotfooted it to the other side of the world, he'd still remember her taste, her touch, her smile.

Molly read the discomfort on Weaver's face and the resignation in his gaze. She sighed. "Geez, Louise." She dumped her brush in the paint can and gave

Weaver a squinty-eyed glare. "It's time we killed the elephant in the living room."

He blinked at her, clearly astonished. "Huh?"

With a burst of breath, Molly blew an annoying strand of hair from her eyes. "I'm going to generously and completely accept responsibility for it, and then you're going to help me kill the annoying thing."

His voice rose an octave. "Huh?"

Molly crossed her arms over her chest. "We have a problem. We haven't talked about it. We even tried to pretend it doesn't exist." She lifted one hand. "So, voilà."

The crease between his eyebrows deepened. He made a pale imitation of her hand gesture. "Voilà?"

"And so the elephant in the living room was born."

The crease between his brows smoothed out.

"You see?" she said. "And it grew, and grew, and grew with every hour we didn't address the problem."

"Which is...?" he inquired warily.

"The problem is...we exchanged a kiss." At his raised eyebrows, she hastened to continue. "Well, okay, more than one."

His eyebrows lowered. "Right."

"And we didn't have any business kissing. Right?"

"Right."

She wished he'd respond with more than one syllable at a time, but at least he was agreeing. "So," she continued, "as I see it, we have three options."

His eyebrows lifted again. "Well?"

She held up a finger. "I could quit."

"No!" He emphatically shook his head. "Next?"

Another finger up. "We could go on tiptoeing around that great big elephant in the living room."

He shook his head again. "Third?"

"We could try to become comfortable with each other. Become friends instead of thinking so much about being...something else."

His mouth twisted wryly. "Friends." He sounded skeptical.

"You never can have too many friends," she said quickly. "You know that."

"So you're sure that if we become friends, we won't be bothered by the...other stuff?"

She wasn't sure of anything of the kind, but they both didn't want her quitting, and her nerves couldn't stand another hour of trying to ignore the elephant. "Sure." She waved away all of his concerns. "Has happened to me dozens of times."

His eyebrows rose. "You've been in this situation dozens of times?"

Heat surged up Molly's neck. "Sure." In for a penny, in for a pound.

He crossed his arms over his chest. "So how do we go about becoming...friendly?" His gaze narrowed on her again, and she felt it like the brush of a fingertip against her cheek.

She gulped. "Well," she said, grabbing up her abandoned paintbrush, thinking quickly. "Maybe we talk a little bit about ourselves."

The corners of his mouth kicked up and he took a step closer to her. "I already know everything about you. You're a schoolteacher. You like dogs and babies. You have a close-knit family, you like to garden, and you want a home."

She had an inkling that he was laughing at her. "Listen, if you're not buying this friends thing, then *you* try to think of something better."

He held up his hands in surrender. "I'm just wondering what else we could learn about each other."

His closeness was making her nervous. She dipped her brush and walked away from him, back to the fence. "I don't know nearly as much about you. Where did you grow up?"

"Not anyplace like this," he said matter-of-factly. "I lived in foster homes since I was two days old."

Her grip tightened on the paintbrush. *A foster child?* "Oh?"

Emotion stayed out of his voice. "My parents dumped me on social services, then disappeared."

"Oh." Molly turned. She wanted to warm him, to bring some animation to his face. Her feet moved toward him. "But you had some family. Your cousin, Daisy's father."

Weaver shrugged. "Can't really call him family, you know. I mean, we were related, of course, but I didn't even know he existed until I was eighteen."

She made herself take a long breath while she carefully balanced her brush on the paint can. "But he came looking for you."

"Yeah. From somewhere he got this strong drive to find relations, blood ties. I never asked him why."

Another long breath filled her lungs. "You never thought it would be nice to find someone to belong to?" She put her hand on his forearm. "You didn't want a family?"

Weaver stared straight in her eyes, his expression serious, a little sad, even. "It's not a question of want, Molly." One long finger tucked a strand of hair behind her ear.

She shivered. "What do you mean?" Her voice came out hoarse.

"I told you. I'm not a 'honey-I'm-home' type of guy. I don't know the first thing about having a family." He stroked the hair back again.

Molly cleared her throat, determined to keep the emotion from her voice. "I don't think it's a knowing thing, Weaver." She laid her palm against his cheek. "It's a *feeling* thing."

He stiffened and a frown drew his brows together in a V. "Never mind," he said. "I don't even know why we're talking about this."

Molly reached up to stroke the dark wing of his hair. "Because we're friends. And as your friend, I'd like to tell you—"

His hand caught hers, his blue eyes silenced her. He rubbed her palm down the prickly stubble of his jaw to his lips. "That's right," he said, his voice deepening. "Friends. Good ol' option three."

His gaze mesmerized her. "Mmm-hmm. Friends," she said. A distinctly unfriendlike heat traveled from his skin to hers. Molly thought about pulling her hand away.

His lips brushed her fingers, darting shivers up her arm.

She stopped thinking.

"But there's a fourth option, Molly."

She could barely hear him over the sound of her heartbeat in her ears. "Fourth option? What fourth option?"

"We could become..."

Anticipation dried her lips. She licked them. "Become what?"

"Lovers," he said.

6

"Yahoo! Hello! Anybody home?"

The sound of a woman's voice reached Weaver at
the same instant he registered Molly backing away.

"Dana!" A note of surprise in her voice, Molly
brushed past Weaver and ran toward the side gate.
"We're in the back."

Feeling as though the governor's call had arrived
in time, Weaver watched Molly embrace a tiny
woman with wavy curls and a big smile. They laugh-
ingly parted when Patch dashed from his spot in the
shade and wedged between them.

"Why did you come?" Molly asked her friend.

And thank God you did, Weaver thought. *Before I
made another stupid move.*

Dana grinned. "I came to meet the new man in
your life."

Silence dropped like a lead weight. Molly pulled
on the hem of her T-shirt, hard. "New man?" she
repeated.

New man? Had Molly's friend overheard his crazy
suggestion and—

"Patch." Dana knelt on the grass at pooch level. "Didn't you say his name is Patch?" She stroked the animal's furry head. "I hope he has more staying power than most of the men in your life."

Molly giggled. Weaver stared at her. He'd never heard such a sound come from her. A giggle. A *nervous* giggle.

"Of course, Patch. Patch is my new man." Another little giggle escaped, then she clapped her hand over her mouth.

Dana rose and turned toward Weaver. "And you are—?" She held out her hand. "I'm Molly's oldest and best friend, Dana Hartley."

Weaver extended his hand and received a brief, but firm handshake. "I'm Weaver Reed," he said. "Molly's, um, uh—" He couldn't think how to describe himself. *Not the new man in her life.*

"Employer?" Dana offered.

His gaze swiveled toward Molly, hers to his. "No," they said together.

"We're—" Weaver broke off again. He couldn't say *friends.*

The two women apparently gave up on him. With an overbright smile, Molly dragged Dana toward the house to show off the baby. From the conversation that floated back to him, Weaver gathered that Dana was a new mother, that her own baby girl was at home with the baby's father, and that Molly had been "way too quiet" about what was going on in her life.

Weaver ran a hand through his hair. *Damn me.*

What was going on in Molly's life was that he was messing it up. Instead of latching on to Molly's notion of friendship, he'd brought up *lovers.*

Weaver speared both hands through his hair. Why was everything backfiring on him? Here he was, just your average Joe, trying to live his own life, and what happens?

Mr. No-Commitments inherits a house and a baby.

City boy finds himself in the suburbs.

Confirmed bachelor shares quarters with a sexy, family-oriented woman.

He groaned.

A warm weight pressed against his legs and Patch gave his hand a sympathetic lick. Weaver glanced down at the dog.

Toothy grin. A look that seemed to say, *What's wrong with a house and a baby?*

What's wrong with a little grass and a neighborhood fleet of minivans?

And with an insistent whine: *What's wrong with Molly?*

Weaver groaned, longer. "What's wrong is that I don't know the first thing about handling any of them." The dog's ears felt like warm butter against his fingers. "I tried it before and it didn't work."

It's not a knowing thing, it's a feeling *thing.* Patch pressed harder against his knees.

Weaver remembered those were Molly's words, too. "You're way too smart for a dog."

And for a man, you're…

An idiot. Weaver could finish that one for himself, easily.

Dana and Molly emerged from the house, Daisy Ann cradled in Molly's arms. Weaver ignored how right they looked together.

"Leaving already?" he asked Dana, who fished her keys from her purse.

She nodded. "Just a quick check on my friend here. I need to get back to Alan and the baby."

Weaver made the mistake of looking at Molly again, then couldn't break his gaze away from the Madonna-and-child pull of her with Daisy in her arms. Even running shorts and a T-shirt advertising a fun run couldn't dampen the maternal glow.

"Nice meeting you," he said, forcing his attention on Dana.

"My husband would enjoy meeting *you*." A gleam entered Dana's eyes. "Hey, we're free for dinner tonight. We could have a barbecue."

"Uh, Daisy..." Weaver hesitated. In his mood, a suburban barbecue was the last form of entertainment he needed.

"We just declared her completely cured, so it's time the two little girls made friends," Dana said.

Molly's face was stiff. "Dana—"

"Oh, come on. We'll have it here so you won't even have to take Daisy out of the house." Dana smiled brilliantly. "What do you say, Weaver? It'll just be a casual thing among friends."

Friends. That word again.

Weaver suddenly pictured them all in the yard. Burgers and chips and soft drinks. Something to think about this afternoon besides Molly. People to be around tonight besides Molly.

Suddenly, it sounded like a fine idea.

"Okay," he slowly agreed. "We'll make potato salad." After two minutes he'd be bored out of his gourd. *Perfect.*

"Potato salad? Which one of the 'we' is going to make potato salad?" Molly looked at him as if he were crazy.

Oh, no, Molly. My sanity is finally returning.

"It'll be, um…fun." A boring suburban barbecue would remind him of all the reasons he and Molly could be nothing more than friends.

Late afternoon, Molly used the butcher knife to push a newly chopped pile of celery toward the mound of diced hard-boiled eggs on the cutting board.

On the countertop to her left, Daisy sat contentedly in her infant seat. Weaver rummaged in the walk-in pantry for paper plates and plastic cutlery. He stepped out, a stack of white rounds in his hands. "I'll take these to the backyard."

Then he escaped. He'd been avoiding her since Dana's unexpected visit. Or, more precisely, since that option four couldn't-we-be-lovers suggestion.

Molly sighed and guillotined an onion, wishing she could cut through her confusion just as easily. What confusion? she admonished herself. They'd agreed to be friends. But...

Calling someone friend didn't make his blue eyes fade, or his hair shine less, or his firm jaw stop pleading for the touch of her hand.

Calling someone friend didn't erase her memory of the silly faces that someone made to amuse a grumpy baby. Or the strange sense of rightness she felt in his arms.

Calling someone friend could just about be the biggest joke of all time.

Daisy gurgled, catching Molly's attention. The baby stared, fascinated, at her own intricately woven fingers. Molly smiled faintly. It was going to be bad enough saying goodbye to Daisy, but on top of that she'd have to suffer lust withdrawal from Weaver, as well.

The combination might just about do her in.

Daisy gurgled again, her head now turned toward the clear bowl of gleaming red strawberries Molly had sliced. "Red," she said to the baby. "Like fire engines and Santa's suit. Pretty, like Daisy Ann and—"

"You."

Molly whirled at the sound of Weaver's voice. A stain of a different red crossed his cheekbones and he looked as surprised at his comment as she was.

He cleared his throat. "Anything more I can do for you?"

Molly licked her dry lips. "Absolutely not," she reminded herself.

He moved to stand in front of Daisy and picked up the bowl, holding it so Daisy had a better view. The baby gurgled again, and Weaver laughed with her.

Molly tore her gaze away from the pair. "I hope you like strawberry shortcake," she said.

"Love it. But I thought women always wanted something chocolate." He'd set down the bowl, and Daisy's little hand was wrapped around one of his strong, long fingers.

"Not me. I cured my addiction years ago."

Still clutching Weaver's hand, Daisy smiled gaily into his face. "How so?" he asked, running his free palm over the fuzz on top of the baby's head.

Molly thought about his hand sweeping over her own hair, trailing over her bare skin. Her heart squeezed, pushing all the oxygen from her lungs. She gulped in air. "I binged myself out of it."

"How'd you do that?" His head turned her way, and he smiled.

The smile hit her like the force of a thousand magnets. Atoms of attraction, pulling her, drawing her, making her want...him. "When I was fifteen, I spent a whole weekend eating it. Chocolate doughnuts. Chocolate ice cream. Chocolate cheesecake. You-name-it chocolate, I ate it twice."

"Whoa. You're not kidding."

She nodded. "Cured myself of chocolate cravings forever."

"Sounds crazy, but I guess it worked." He smiled again.

"I guess it did." She could hardly breathe again.

As if he sensed her tension, he abruptly stepped backward. "I think I'll go...do something."

He brushed past her, and the tiny hairs on her skin rose as if to follow him. She sighed. Her addiction to Weaver seemed as strong as the one she'd once had for chocolate.

Clack. The sound of the butcher knife dropping to the cutting board punctuated the intriguing thought that flew into her head.

Could she get rid of her lust for Weaver the same way she'd overcome her lust for chocolate?

Goose bumps spread over her skin. Could she binge herself free of Weaver? Could becoming his lover cure her of him forever?

Weaver assumed the barbecue would be a snooze fest. He expected two couples and two infants would incite enough yawns in him to swallow up any wayward desire he had for babies, dogs and family-oriented women. By the goodbyes, he'd be able to handle the intimacy of the darkness alone with Molly. He could be her friend.

Sure, after this little dinnertime reminder of how little they had in common, how much her kind of life didn't suit him, darkness with Molly would be a breeze.

Just as he'd gotten this line of thinking down pat, she blindsided him two minutes before the guests were due to arrive. With quick steps, she carried to the backyard a patchwork quilt. She wore a tank top and a miniskirt, which, when she turned around, he discovered was actually a pair of shorts.

Feeling noble, he contemplated the mysteries of female fashion instead of watching her bend to spread the quilt on the shaded grass beside the patio. Then she straightened, bit her lip and shot him an assessing look.

She bit her lip again and nervously tucked a strand of hair behind her ear. "I've been thinking about that option four you mentioned."

He choked on his own gasp.

"Are you okay?" She came toward him.

He held her off with a hastily thrown-up hand. "You didn't say what I think you did." A statement, not a question.

"If you think I suggested we might become lovers, then I did say it." She rubbed her palms against her skirt-shorts thing.

Drawing his attention to her long legs. The ones that night after night he'd fantasized about being wrapped around his waist. *Oh, my God.*

The doorbell rang before his mind could speed up, or slow down, or whatever it needed to do to make sense of all this. "Why'd you bring this up now?" he asked, hardly recognizing the hoarse and cracked voice that came out of his throat.

She blinked, her silver eyes serious. "To give you time to think about it." Her head turned toward the

The Editor's "Thank You" Free Gifts Include:

- Four BRAND-NEW romance novels!
- A lovely Cherub Magnet!

PLACE
FREE GIFT
SEAL
HERE

YES! I have placed my Editor's "Thank You" seal in the space provided above. Please send me 4 free books and a beautiful Cherub Magnet. I understand I am under no obligation to purchase any books, as explained on the back and on the opposite page.

201 CIS CA9Q (U-SIL-YT-09/97)

Name _____

Address _____ Apt. _____

City _____

State _____ Zip _____

Thank You!

DETACH AND MAIL CARD TODAY!

The Silhouette Reader Service™ — Here's How It Works:

Accepting free books places you under no obligation to buy anything. You may keep the books and gift and return the shipping statement marked "cancel." If you do not cancel, about a month later we will send you 4 additional novels, and bill you just $2.69 each plus 25¢ delivery per book and applicable sales tax, if any.* That's the complete price, and—compared to cover prices of $3.50 each—quite a bargain! You may cancel at any time, but if you choose to continue, every other month we'll send you 4 more books, which you may either purchase at the discount price...or return to us and cancel your subscription.
*Terms and prices subject to change without notice. Sales tax applicable in N.Y.

If offer card is missing write to: The Silhouette Reader Service, 3010 Walden Ave., P.O. Box 1867, Buffalo, NY 14240-1867

BUSINESS REPLY MAIL
FIRST-CLASS MAIL   PERMIT NO. 717   BUFFALO, NY

POSTAGE WILL BE PAID BY ADDRESSEE

SILHOUETTE READER SERVICE
3010 WALDEN AVE
PO BOX 1867
BUFFALO NY 14240-9952

NO POSTAGE
NECESSARY
IF MAILED
IN THE
UNITED STATES

sound of the second ring of the doorbell. "We can discuss the idea later. I'll go let them in."

To give me time to think about it? He thought about wringing her neck. He thought about running, screaming crazily, into the night. He thought mostly about sending this nice, boring couple on their way and then dragging Molly off to his bed.

But the nice, boring couple were already in his backyard, setting down bowls of food and six-packs and baby paraphernalia. Their little baby—cute little thing named Camille—was quickly ensconced beside Daisy Ann on the quilt Molly had laid on the grass.

Alan Hartley, Dana's husband, liked microbrewery beer and to sit near his wife and baby. He watched them with a faint, besotted smile on his face, as if they'd been put on this earth for his unceasing delight.

The other man gave Weaver a much needed feeling of relief. He had nothing in common with this guy. Thanks to Molly—don't look at her pretty, tempting face, he cautioned himself—it was up to Weaver alone to resist getting any closer. Alan Hartley was going to help him do it.

A baby's laugh drew his attention. Molly sat on the quilt with Daisy against her, tickling the little girl with the paintbrush end of her long, dark braid. Daisy kept trying to catch it in her pudgy hands, and for the first time, Weaver noticed the unbelievable perfection of the baby's fingernails. And then Molly laughed, and he found himself fascinated by the wink of the earrings in her lobes. He'd never seen her wear jew-

elry before, and he imagined her taking them out that
night before she went to bed....

*I've been thinking about that option four you men-
tioned.*

Oh, no. To turn off the thought and refocus on their
differences, he escaped in the direction of the pro-
pane-fueled grill. Like the lawn mower, it had a
beastly aspect to it and he welcomed the unpleasant
challenge.

The control panel looked like something NASA
dreamed up.

After several baffled minutes, a familiar perfume
floated by his nose. He looked over his shoulder at
Molly, who gripped a platter of hamburger patties.
"We can either roast meat or launch rockets with this
thing," he said. "And I don't have a clue which does
what."

*See, honey? There's no way in hell we should be
together.*

She laughed, apparently oblivious to his silent mes-
sage.

He tried again. "I can disassemble and assemble
an assault rifle in six seconds. I know karate and tae
kwan do." He crossed his arms over his chest. "But
I don't have the slightest idea how to get this thing
going."

"There you go," she said. "You're right. These
suburbs are trickier than life in the spy-burbs."

"I'm not too good with barbecues myself." Alan's

deep voice sounded on Weaver's left. "Can't always keep control of the flames."

Weaver groaned inwardly as Molly ran a supposedly reassuring, yet definitely heat-inducing palm down his forearm. "He's not kidding, you know. And he's a fireman." She walked back—thank God—to Dana and the babies.

Weaver forced his attention to Alan. *A fireman?* He'd pegged the man as an engineer or accountant or something. Not because Alan looked as if he pushed a pencil, necessarily, but it just seemed like the kind of job for a guy who so obviously doted on his wife and child.

"Surprised you?" Alan grinned and reached down to twist one of several dials. Then he told Weaver to press the red button on the right side of the panel.

Flames roared. Weaver leapt back, a hand rubbing at what he imagined were the remains of his eyebrows. It took a moment for his pulse to subside to prebonfire speed. Dull, he reminded himself, you're finding this deadly dull.

Alan handed Weaver a spatula, and he began to load the burgers onto the grill. The flames leapt toward them and a satisfying aroma curled toward his nose.

Meat on the grill, Weaver crossed to the cooler and got out a couple more cold beers. He handed one of the sweating bottles to Alan and the two of them watched the flames.

But the surprising satisfaction of conquering another suburban animal couldn't keep his mind off Molly's mind-blowing offer.

"Have you known Molly long?" he asked Alan.

The other guy nodded. "I met her five years ago, on the same night I met my wife."

At Weaver's raised eyebrows, Alan continued, a reminiscent smile creeping over his face. "At a cantina across the border, famous for tequila and Mexican beer. Those two were drinking virgin daiquiris and flipping pesos for designated-driver status."

Alan slugged back a mouthful of beer. "I took them under my protection."

A cool finger of concern jabbed Weaver. "They were in some kind of danger?"

"Yeah. From dangerous leerers and dangerous gropers." Alan grinned. "I wasn't half as bad as the other guys. I might have leered, but I never groped."

Weaver ran his thumb over the wet bottle of beer, inspecting the clean swipe he made on the glass. "Molly still needs rescuing."

"From you?"

Yes. He was wrong for her. But he couldn't bring himself to say it aloud. Just as he couldn't admit how much he liked the warm suburban evening air or the company, or the sound of feminine laughter wafting across the patio.

To avoid answering, he looked toward the women, flanking the two babies on the quilt. Another laugh rose up, then suddenly baby Camille burped.

Her father laughed. "Way to go, woman," he

called out. "She belches like a sailor." He shot a proud grin at Weaver.

Weaver tried letting the paternal comment pass. Failed. He held up an often infant-captured thumb. "Daisy's got a grip like King Kong's."

Alan appeared unimpressed. "When Camille's hungry, she's louder than Howard Stern."

"Daisy's hair is as blond as Dennis Rodman's—"

"Was last week," Alan finished for him. They exchanged grins and let the one-upmanship die while they finished their beers and watched the babies. Daisy's Rodman do ruffled in the breeze as her chubby legs bicycled and her arms waved.

He spoke more to himself than Alan. "She's not really mine, you know." That's why he couldn't have her. In the distant, dark past, he'd tried taking on fatherhood. Tried and failed. "Not like Camille is yours."

The other man shrugged, took another swig. "I suppose it could make a difference," he said, his voice neutral.

Weaver buried the uncomfortable moment by turning his attention to the burgers. He didn't let himself think of anything—Daisy or Molly—until they all sat down to the meal, the babies content in side-by-side infant seats.

Dinner progressed smoothly enough, though Weaver discovered, ironically, that Dana's stories as a psychologist, Alan's as a firefighter and Molly's as a teacher could be as hair-raising and infinitely more humorous than his. At one point, he laughed so hard at Molly's description of first-grade "cootie" wars that she came around the table to pound him on the back.

Her arm stayed around his shoulders as his coughing quieted. "You okay?" she asked. Her fingers brushed the hair at his nape.

He stilled, afraid she'd remove her fingers, afraid she wouldn't. "I'm terrible," he answered in all honesty. He shot a look at Dana and Alan, who had gathered up the dishes and were heading toward the kitchen. "I'm supposed to be having a terrible time."

A frown puckered her brows. "I—"

He put his fingers against her soft mouth. "Don't try to figure it out."

His fingers slid away, but she put her own hand to her mouth, as if holding his touch there.

He groaned. The battle was being lost, fast. At this rate, he wouldn't even wait for the other couple to leave before taking Molly in his arms again. "Molly." Without volition, he turned his chair and grabbed her hands. "This isn't right." A distant ring couldn't stop his momentum. "This is crazy."

"This phone call is for you." Alan came toward him, holding out the portable phone.

Gut tight, Weaver grabbed the phone, the voice on the other end twisting his tension higher. He punched the off button and gripped the receiver, hard.

"I've got to go," he told Molly. "Emergency strategy meeting." The Czech situation had come to a head, and as the one in charge of the mission before he'd left Maryland, he had to attend.

Staring down at his white-knuckled hand, he waited for the feelings of relief. Back to work! Reprieve from the 'burbs!

He kept waiting.

Molly drew his gaze as she made a quick, jerky movement toward the baby. She picked up Daisy Ann and held her tightly. The baby smiled.

Weaver's insides gave another sharp twist. Shouldn't he be glad to leave this? "I'll be back, of course. Probably tomorrow." *But just temporarily.*

Eventually none of this, neither Molly nor Daisy, would be his.

"We'll be here," she said, her voice quiet.

He spun away, anxious to get going. Then something—something beyond his control—made him turn back. His hand reached toward Daisy, stroked her plump cheek. He didn't let himself touch Molly.

But the unreadable look in her silver eyes haunted him.

Just after 6:00 a.m., Weaver unlocked the front door. Immediately, the house's familiar smell filled his nose and cleared his head. His tension ebbed away and he repressed an impulse to call out, "I'm home."

The emergency meeting had been hastily assembled in Los Angeles for Weaver's convenience. They'd been forced to pick another team for the Czech job since he was tied up. Though not his first choice, Sonia and Harry were well trained and had all the background he'd gathered.

He could've spent the rest of the night in L.A., but after the meeting broke, he'd driven south.

Clink. Clatter. Clank. Patch rushed down the hallway to greet him. "Sh, boy, sh." Weaver patted the dog. He'd actually taken a hotel room, but he'd suddenly detested its cold temperature and empty closet.

And no matter what, the room couldn't smell like ho—*here*—a soothing combination of Daisy's powder and Molly's perfume.

And it hadn't held the two females he couldn't get off his mind.

Ignoring the urge to look in on them, he went to his room, threw off his clothes and pulled on sweatpants. God, he needed sleep. After some z's, the entire evening would fall into perspective: the barbecue boring, the meeting vital, Daisy Ann an encumbrance, Molly undesirable.

Just a little sleep. He flopped on the bed and closed his eyes. Molly's scent filled his head, Daisy's laugh his ears.

Sleep, he commanded himself.

Molly again. Then Daisy—

Daisy's very real whimper.

Good. Nothing like a middle-of-the-night baby cry for a little perspective.

He jumped out of bed, eager to reach the baby before Molly awoke and he had to face her, too.

On her back in her crib, Daisy Ann blinked up at

him. He changed her diaper. Then he pulled up her blanket, preparing to leave her again. Hesitating, he peered into her face. The baby didn't look sleepy. As a matter of fact, she looked as if she didn't want to be alone. As if she'd work herself up into a sleep-shattering wail if he left her that way.

And the wail would wake Molly, which would wake his libido, which would kibosh the whole perspective thing. "Sh," he said quietly. "Daisy Ann, sh."

She made tiny baby grunts as he picked her up, then cradled her against his chest. He tiptoed out the door and down the hall to the living room—the farthest point in the house from the office Molly used as a bedroom. "Sh," he said one more time, against the baby's soft hair. "Let's not wake up Molly."

Jingle-clank. Patch's collar rattled metallically as Weaver slid onto the couch. The dog moved from his sleeping spot by the fireplace to crowd Weaver's legs. He reached a hand down and rubbed the dog's ears. "Hey, friend. You and Daisy both looking for a little company this morning?"

The baby gazed solemnly up at him, not a trace of drowsiness in her eyes. Her forehead creased, she wriggled, and then gave a bored grumble. Weaver shifted, snuggling her more comfortably in the crook of his elbow. "You need a bedtime story, little girl?"

Daisy quieted, smiled up at him. When he didn't say any more, her forehead creased again, deeper this time, and her grumbles became more plaintive.

"Hey, hey, hey," Weaver protested softly, glancing down the dark hall. "We don't want to wake anybody, remember?"

When his voice subsided, Daisy wriggled more, groused louder. Patch whimpered and shifted restlessly.

"Okay, okay." He gently tapped the baby's nose. "I'll keep talking." With a contented groan, Patch flopped back down, his chin on Weaver's bare feet.

Weaver shook his head. "Oh, man. This is the life. Sandwiched between a hot-breathed dog and an insomniac infant."

Daisy gurgled. Patch let out a wet sigh that misted Weaver's toes.

"Pleasant," he said, afraid to stop talking. "But no lullabies," he murmured. "I'll spare us all that pain."

Patch sighed again, obviously relieved.

"What can I talk about?" He looked deeply into the baby's eyes. "Spying? Nah, top secret. The military? Four words. Steer clear of leathernecks."

He rested his head against the couch. "What next? I don't know anything about ballet, or Barbies, or anything else a girl needs to know." Grimacing, he opened his eyes. "Men." He shifted Daisy Ann so she had a better view of his face. "I suppose I could tell you about men."

Moving silently down the dark hall on bare feet, Molly paused at Weaver's words. A large shot of laughter bubbled inside her, mixed with her relief that he was back already, and safe. A little smile played over her lips. Weaver Reed on men? At the arched entry to the living room she sank to the oriental hall runner.

Now *this* was something worth waking up for.

7

Weaver leaned back against the couch, keeping his voice low and soothing. Daisy Ann gazed at him, trust in her eyes.

"Men." He paused, gathering his thoughts. The baby squirmed. "Let's see." Talking again quieted her immediately. "There's always the basics. Don't meet a blind date in a private place. Don't go anywhere with a man unless you have cab fare in your pocket. And don't dance too close. That's not just a stiff zipper he's got there, you know."

Patch snorted his impatience over Weaver's feet.

He slanted a look at the dog. "Okay, you're right. Dear Abby can tell her all that stuff. But she wants me to keep talking. I'm no sage."

Gaze glued to his face, Daisy Ann ignored his doubts and nestled her little body in the crook of his arm. Her weight against his chest seemed to ease the weight of responsibility on his shoulders. He breathed deeply, easily. Deeper and easier than he had in a long time.

What if… He couldn't quite formulate the thought, though his arms cuddled her possessively. Maybe…

Daisy Ann blew a frivolous spit bubble, and the innocence of the act clawed at his gut. He couldn't risk a maybe when it came to Daisy Ann. "Now, listen, Daisy. There's one thing about men I *am* sure about. There's a segment of the male gender, I don't know, maybe twenty percent of us, who are capable of breaking your heart."

She blew another bubble that popped, dissolved. Didn't seem to concern her.

"Just like that, Daisy. Bubble today, gone tomorrow. We just can't do the family thing."

She reached out for his nose, squeezed in retaliation.

He pried her starfish fingers off. "It's nothing personal. It's not that your blue eyes and baby hands aren't the cutest I've ever seen and all that."

She smiled, gurgled.

He tried ignoring the flirtation. "What am I doing?" he asked himself. "I'm supposed to be talking about men in general, not me in particular. But…"

His silence bothered her again. She grumbled in protest.

"But you're not really mine," Weaver said, the words leaking out.

Her movements stilled.

"I feel responsible for you, don't get me wrong, but I feel responsible for you getting the very best."

Her hand reached toward him again, patted his chin, his mouth.

"We Reeds have had the worst. Your dad, me, your mom even. Never had good luck when it comes to family. And look at you. Lost both your folks in one fell swoop."

Instead of listening, Daisy let her fingers swoop over to grab his ear. He leaned forward to accommodate her.

She gripped tightly.

"Let me go, Daisy." But Weaver said the words without any conviction. He inhaled, breathing in her powder scent, the fragrance of the golden baby shampoo he'd seen Molly spread over the little girl's scalp the afternoon before. "Let me go, Daisy."

Her other hand came up and twined in the short hairs at his temple. She wasn't about to let him get away.

"Honey," Weaver said. "What do you want from me?" He swallowed to lubricate his hoarse voice.

She hung on silently.

"I wish I could have you." He sucked in air. "Okay, is that what you wanted to hear? Because it's true. I wish I could have you. I wish I knew what to do with you, how to raise you, some way I could make you my little girl."

Her hands released him, and she smiled contentedly.

"But it doesn't mean it can happen, Daisy."

Her happy expression didn't falter.

"Daisy, it won't happen."

Her eyelashes landed to rest on her plump cheeks, and she dived back into slumber like a peaceful star falling from the sky.

Molly pulled her light robe closer and hugged her knees. To see—well, listen to, actually—Weaver admit he wanted Daisy Ann thrilled her. Last night when he'd left, Dana claimed she'd seen doubt and regret in his eyes. Molly had read something new there, too—but experience made her cautious to even name it, let alone believe in it.

Weaver had quit speaking, but she stayed hidden in the hallway, not the least bit guilty for eavesdropping and not willing to miss anything else he might say. She'd sat there in the first place, ready to be amused and entertained by Weaver's insights into his own gender, only to hear instead his own wishes.

He wanted Daisy Ann for his little girl.

Well, who wouldn't? The baby was a sweetheart, and Molly herself hadn't been able to resist her charms. In Weaver's case, Daisy was more, she was family, and she needed him.

Weaver should have realized that from the beginning!

A chill of unease raised the flesh on her arms. Of course, he didn't seem absolutely convinced he should raise Daisy. Molly didn't understand why, but it seemed Weaver thought loneliness to be his lot in life.

They needed to talk. Not about the two of them—any lingering consideration of option four paled to ghost pallor in comparison to Weaver's relationship with Daisy Ann. But if she approached him now, tired and vulnerable, maybe she could get him to abandon this idea of giving Daisy Ann to someone else.

Patch's collar rattled a warning and Molly rose silently.

Weaver's voice mumbled, "Sorry, old boy, but Daisy's asleep, and my feet are getting there, thanks to your chin. Let's all go back to bed."

Back to bed? She wouldn't sleep a wink. And if she let Weaver go, he'd have a chance to rebuild his rock-solid defenses. Weaver needed love and family in his life and she knew now was the right time to make him see that.

He just needed to confess to her that he loved Daisy Ann.

Determined to make that happen, Molly retreated to her room and then came innocently wandering from it when she spied Weaver emerging from Daisy Ann's.

He stopped short. "Did I wake you?" he asked quietly.

She pulled tight on the belt of her robe. A pair of sweatpants rode low on Weaver's hips. His chest was bare. Tanned, muscled and bare. His nipples, flat bronze disks, suddenly fascinated her.

"Molly?" He came forward, put a hand on her

shoulder. "You okay?" His fingers gripped firmly and shook her a little.

She stepped away from his touch. "I'm fine." Her smile wobbled a bit. She was supposed to be thinking about his home life, not her hormones! "I just woke up a little...hungry."

Heat traveled up her neck. She hoped in the dimness he wouldn't see it and absolutely hoped he didn't pick up on her double entendre.

"Hungry?" His eyes narrowed and he stepped closer.

She stepped back. *His home life*, she told herself. *You're supposed to be working on him to admit he loves Daisy Ann.* "Are there any cornflakes left? Milk?" Something cold.

His shoulders relaxed. "Yeah. In the fridge, of course." He moved to walk past her. "G'night."

"Good night?" The words squeaked out of her throat. She'd expected him to follow her to the kitchen.

He halted again. "It's too early in the morning for me, Molly. I'm going to bed."

"You're not hun— You don't want some cereal, too?" She congratulated herself on the quick save.

"Nah."

What could she do? Frustrated, she watched him stride down the hallway and disappear behind his door.

"Oh, heck."

As if sensing her distress, Patch ambled out of Daisy's half-open door and jingled down the hall toward her. She stroked his soft head.

With a sigh, Molly headed for the kitchen and turned on the light. She didn't really want anything to eat, of course, but she figured she better get a bowl out and make some signs of interest in it.

She stubbed her toe on the hard, cold kickplate of the refrigerator. She hopped up and down, gripping her sore toe in one hand. Darn it all, Weaver's heart would be just as hard and cold by morning. No way could she give up him now, when he was vulnerable.

The only one enthusiastic for the cereal was Patch. She let him slurp down the milk, followed by a dog biscuit chaser. As she shut the pantry door, her gaze fell on the big spider she'd been watching for the past couple of days. Molly, who regarded herself of the live-and-let-live yet down-with-all-flies school, had allowed the eight-legger to build an intricate, yet unobtrusive web in the corner of the kitchen window.

Lucky that Dana hadn't spotted the bug. She despised the things, had even been known to wake Alan out of a sound sleep to kill—

Aha.

Okay, so it wasn't the most imaginative ploy. "But desperate times and all that," she told the chomping Patch.

It only took her a couple of seconds to retrace her steps and knock lightly on Weaver's door.

"What do you need?" He didn't sound the least bit sleepy, she thought gratefully.

"There's a bug."

"A bug?" Apparently he didn't see the connection.

She hated being the one to make it for him. "Um, uh, men kill bugs."

"What do women do with them?"

"It's a big, big spider."

Disbelief infused his voice. "You want me to kill it for you?"

She couldn't make herself admit to it. She thought of all the women she'd be disserving if she did. "I want you to come into the kitchen," she said truthfully.

Thank goodness he didn't grumble. Thank goodness he didn't quiz her on her insect fear. Instead, he just appeared in the doorway, sexy in sweatpants again—*sigh*—and followed her without comment to the kitchen.

Poor spider. It didn't stand a chance. Before she could even suggest its removal to the yard, Weaver flattened it with the palm of his hand.

She made sure he washed both of them afterward.

And then he tried to get away from her again.

"Where you going?" she squeaked out once more.

He looked over one strong, heavy shoulder. "Back to bed."

Now what? "Don't you—are you sure you wouldn't like some cereal?"

His eyes narrowed, as they had in the hall, as if he suspected something. But then he shrugged, poured himself a bowlful and sat down at the kitchen table.

She scooted to the place opposite him, crossed her arms over her chest, then cleared her throat. He didn't look up. She cleared her throat again. "I thought maybe we could talk."

His gaze flicked her way. "It's not a good time, Molly. I'm tired—"

"That's what makes it so perfect. We'll get to the heart of the matter right away." *Don't scare him off.* "So to speak," she added hastily.

His hand left his bowl and reached across to grasp hers. His fingertips were cool. "My resistance is down, Molly."

The husky note in his voice rubbed across her skin and her fingers tightened on his. "That's the whole point," she admitted. "I don't want you resisting."

"No? You're sure?" At her nod, his grip tightened and he leaned toward her, his mouth pressing the side of her jaw. His lips cold from the milk. Her skin hot from his nearness.

For some reason she tilted her head, and his mouth, warmed now, slid down her neck. He murmured something against her flesh.

Molly stiffened. This wasn't why she was here! Back primly straight, she pulled away and inched her chair from his proximity.

One of his eyebrows quirked up.

"Talk," she said to the inquiring brow. She didn't look at any other part of him. Too tempting.

"Oh, right. You said you wanted to discuss the idea."

Molly didn't remember those exact words, but close enough. "Right," she said.

To start over, she cleared her throat again. "So, um, Daisy had a little trouble sleeping?"

"Mmm." He watched her closely. "But I don't think she'll be up again. We have at least a few hours." He smiled slowly.

Molly's pulse revved. She checked the bowl between them, expecting he'd made soup from the cereal with the heat of that smile. Her insides certainly were mushy.

She cleared her throat again. "She's sweet, isn't she?"

The corners of his grin kicked up. "'Specially if she stays asleep for a while."

Molly blinked. "Well, sure, that will give us time…"

"We'll need plenty of it." His chair scraped against the floor as he edged toward her. "And just for the record, I'm not tired at all anymore."

Molly blinked again. "Terrific, because we…"

That grin again. "Have a lot to discuss?"

"Of course, um…" This was so surprisingly easy, she was a bit confused.

His hand recaptured hers, and his thumb slid down to her wrist to make distracting circles against her pulse. "I wasn't going to agree, you know. No way, uh-uh, I wasn't going to get involved."

Why was he telling her this? She knew he'd never planned on keeping Daisy. But those little circles kept stroking her pulse and she couldn't quite form the question.

He stared down at their joined hands. "But then the whole drive to L.A. and back, I couldn't get the idea out of my mind." His head suddenly came up. "To tell the truth, I made it back in record time. Lucky for me the highway patrol must've been on a doughnut break."

Molly smiled and squeezed his hand. "You *are* lucky," she said. "For more reasons than that." He'd gained guardianship of the most precious gift in the world!

With his free hand, he tucked a strand of hair around her ear. Then he traced the rim, slowly, sensuously. "Mmm. I know."

His hand moved from her ear to her elbow and he pulled her toward him. "Lucky to have such sweetness land in my lap." And that *was* where she landed.

Molly swallowed and tried ignoring the warmth of his naked chest searing through her light robe. Something was wrong here. Oh, it felt completely right, *hormonally correct*, but weren't they supposed to be discussing something else? "Daisy." That was it.

He nuzzled her neck again. "I told you. Asleep. Down for the count."

"I mean about you deciding to keep her."

His head came up so quickly he smacked her chin with his forehead. "Ouch. What the hell are you talking about?"

"I'm talking about Daisy Ann. How you couldn't

get her out of your mind. How you decided to get involved.'' She rubbed her smarting chin.

He ran a hand over his burgeoning bump. *''What?''*

''Aren't we talking about Daisy Ann?'' Molly asked.

Weaver looked astounded. ''Aren't we talking about option four?''

''Option four?'' Molly heard her voice squeaking again. She'd been thinking... He'd been thinking... Her face heated and she scooted out of his lap and onto her chair. ''I wasn't.''

''You weren't?''

She shook her head.

''You don't want...'' He let the question go unfinished.

''I hadn't thought...'' Not since she'd heard him talking so tenderly to Daisy Ann.

''Well, I have.''

She frowned. ''I don't know.''

''You said you would.''

''I said I wanted to discuss it.'' Her gaze ran from his rumpled hair to his exasperated expression to his wide shoulders and the absolute, stomach-clenching beauty of his bare chest. She put her hands over her eyes. ''I must be going nuts.''

''You and me both.'' He stared at the ceiling, his voice containing her exact bewilderment.

''It's just that I thought we were talking about something else. About how you love Daisy Ann.''

Weaver's gaze whipped from the ceiling to her. "Love Daisy Ann?" Disbelief showed all over his face and his ironic chuckle sounded half-choked. "I wouldn't know how."

Bam. Bam. Bam. Molly's heart pounded against her chest. She had to say something. She had to think of something first. But all she could do was feel the most profound, deepest disappointment in her life.

The phone rang shrilly.

From down the hall, Daisy Ann cried. And Molly stared at Weaver, still stunned.

His grab for the kitchen phone got her legs moving, and zombielike, Molly headed toward the baby.

When she reentered the kitchen, with Daisy in her arms, Weaver was standing beside the sink, his fingers gripping the edge of the countertop.

"Weaver?" Molly wanted to touch him, but she gathered Daisy closer instead.

He turned and walked toward them, as if the baby drew him like a magnet. "Thanks for taking such good care of her."

"My...pleasure." Her throat tightened.

Something was really wrong. Suddenly Weaver halted, then threw himself into one of the kitchen chairs. He slid down to lean his head against its back. "Daisy's okay?" He closed his eyes.

Molly swallowed to wet her dry mouth. "Who was that? Can you—do you want to tell me?"

Weaver didn't open his eyes. "Gabe. He figured we'd be up by seven."

Molly checked the wall clock—yes, 7:00 a.m.— then swallowed. "Did he call—is it something to do with Daisy?" she asked.

"Yeah."

Silence swelled in the room. The hum of the refrigerator took on the annoying whine of an insect buzz. Molly wanted to scream.

"Are you going to tell me?"

He opened his eyes, pain dulling their bright blue. A short laugh escaped him. "You think you want to know?"

Molly gathered Daisy still closer against her. "Tell me."

"Gabe's given up."

A shiver ran down Molly's spine. "Given up?"

"On finding someone from the family to take Daisy Ann."

Molly pressed back against the kitchen wall to suppress another shudder. "Why is that?"

"No one to be found." He shrugged helplessly. "I wanted to find family, a blood relation, because I knew how important that was to Jim. We started by looking for Reeds, since I knew a little about them, but nothing."

Silence again.

Molly licked her lips. "So you were looking for someone on Daisy's mother's side."

"Yeah."

"No one there, either?" Her insides squeezed again, as if a torrent of tears were being released.

"No one." He fisted his hands. "Gabe dead-ended on the very last lead. He suggested I see the lawyer about getting papers."

Another shiver rippled through her. "What kind of papers?"

"The papers I need to put Daisy up for adoption."

Molly stared at him. "You're going to let Daisy go to a *stranger?*"

With a violent gesture, Weaver slammed his palms on the table and jumped up from the chair. "Damn it, Molly, I was just fooling myself. Anyone who adopted Daisy would be a stranger, whether they had some blood tie to her or not."

He strode toward the back door. "Hell, Molly. *I'm* a stranger to her."

Thud. The door slammed shut.

As dusk settled over the neighborhood, Weaver took Daisy Ann for a long walk in the warm evening air. He didn't use the stroller or the jogger but held her high in his arms and spoke quietly into her ear.

"Sorry I flipped out on you earlier today, little one." He grimaced. "Guess I hoped the right people for you would be somewhere in your family tree."

Daisy blinked back at him and blew an air bubble. He felt forgiven.

"What about Molly?" he asked. "Do you think I owe her an apology?"

She'd been strangely silent when he'd returned to the house after his early morning blowup. He'd escaped to the garage for the rest of the day, while she'd puttered about the house. When he'd announced his intention to take Daisy for a walk fifteen minutes ago, she'd merely frowned and said, "See you later," in a distracted voice.

He could tell she disliked the idea of putting Daisy up for adoption.

Molly obviously disliked it so much, he wondered how much longer he would have her in his life.

Would she leave tomorrow? Tonight, maybe? Would she be gone when he returned to the house?

A funny pain stabbed his chest. "We gotta get back, Daisy." He spun around in the direction he'd come. "We just can't let her walk out on us."

You're the one walking out on them. Weaver stomped all over that stupid thought.

Rushing down the streets, dodging cruising cats and stray playground balls, he tried not thinking at all. He didn't want to imagine the house without Molly in it. The quiet without Patch's clanking collar. His future within the absolute, deadly silence of his town house in Maryland, which didn't have a woman, a dog or a baby.

Pain stabbed his chest again, but holding Daisy a little closer seemed to lessen it. "I'm going to do right by you," he promised. "I'll find you that family, Daisy."

And if he was a little bit lonelier at the end of all this?

No. Not lonely. Busy. With his job, and his—his—

The house came into sight. With a wash of relief, he noted the lamps lit in the living room. He could feel Molly inside, her warmth as palpable as the lights.

She sat in the living room, on the corner of the couch, and her head came up when he shut the front door.

"I want to talk to you," she said.

Weaver suppressed his instinctive impulse to head right back out the front door. He didn't want to discuss Daisy's future—hell, anybody's future—right now. "Why, Molly? What's there to talk about?"

She stood up. "Let's put Daisy Ann to bed first. She's asleep."

The fresh air had done Daisy in. He followed Molly to the baby's bedroom and helped her deftly change the baby's diaper and put her into pajamas without waking her.

They both stared down at her once she was on her back in the crib. Molly tenderly pulled up the baby blanket and smoothed it over Daisy's tummy. Weaver made himself look away.

As they left the room, Molly touched his arm. "We need to talk."

He'd never seen Molly so serious. Her silver eyes glowed like polished metal—and her determination seemed as strong.

In the living room again, she took her place on the

couch, and he tried to avoid her gaze by staring at the picture hanging over the mantel.

"You know I wish you'd keep Daisy."

He ignored the now familiar pain in his chest. "You know I can't."

She half smiled. "It's your loss."

"Don't think I don't know it."

"But I'm not willing to lose." Her gaze found him now.

He frowned. "What are you talking about?"

"I'm talking about Daisy. I'm talking about me and Daisy Ann."

He shook his head as if that might clear it. "I'm not following you."

"Weaver, I want to adopt her."

8

Molly searched his face for some pleasure or approval but could only find stunned surprise.

"You want to adopt her." He shook his head again.

"I've thought hard about it. Seriously about it. I want to be Daisy's mother."

He blinked. "Have you thought *long* about it?"

"Only since this morning. Since you said you'd given up on a blood relation." She found the hem of her T-shirt and gripped it hard. "She doesn't need to go to strangers, Weaver. Not when she has me."

He forked a hand through his hair and blinked again, as if he was still trying to understand her words. "I never thought... I never expected..."

"Me, neither. But it seems so right. I went looking for a dog because my maternal urges needed something warm and cuddly to nurture. I not only found Patch, but Daisy Ann, too."

"I don't know." A strange expression crossed his face.

"What's wrong?"

"I need some air." He strode from the room, and she heard the front door open and the screen door click shut. He didn't pause when he returned to the living room. "I'm going to open all the windows."

He left her again.

Molly crossed her arms over her chest, crossed one leg over another. Muted sounds of window sashes rising drifted into the living room. She swung one foot nervously.

Why wouldn't he just answer the question? Why couldn't he just say yes?

The thought of Daisy going up for an anonymous adoption had floored her. And in the instant she'd picked her heart up off the ground, the solution had flowered in her mind. Why shouldn't she? Why couldn't she?

But first, Weaver had to agree. And he hadn't returned.

She listened hard, but the window opening had ceased. A soft breath of warm, perfumed air floated through the living room. The cross breeze made it apparent he'd done his fresh-air bit all the way to the back of the house.

So where was he?

She left the couch and with Patch at her heels, went through the kitchen, family room, looked out to the backyard. He wasn't in the office or his bedroom.

As a last resort, she palmed open the almost shut door to Daisy's room. And found him hovering, looking like a dark and lonely angel, over her bed.

His arms rested against the crib rail and he didn't look up as she came forward.

She moved even closer, her hand reaching out to his shoulder, but then she thought better of touching him. Her fingers landed on the crib railing, grasped it tightly.

"It could be wonderful, Weaver. She'll have grandparents. My mom and dad will dote on her."

"I'm more worried about you."

Her stomach tensed. "I have a degree in education and six years of teaching experience." She paused. "And I love her."

Weaver turned his head and looked at her now. He straightened, one hand reaching out to stroke her hair. "I wasn't worried about your qualifications, Molly. Just about the position I put you in."

She bit her lip. "I'm *asking* for the position, Weaver. You didn't put me here."

He shook his head. "I still feel like I trapped you."

"But you didn't, Weaver. When I came here to adopt Patch, I was looking for something to fill the emptiness in my heart."

"So you got the dog."

"But it wasn't enough." She gripped the crib rail tighter. "And that's why I agreed to be the nanny. Something about Daisy felt so right."

His head turned again, and even in the dim light she felt his gaze fixed on her face.

Her stomach tightened nervously. Swooped and whirled. "Come September I'll be in my own house, but my folks will only be a few miles away. I know they'll give me any support I might need."

He looked back at Daisy. "Courts don't like single-parent adoptions, Molly. There was a case XNS was involved in...the details aren't important. Just that I know it was hell for our single client to adopt the baby we rescued."

Her heart dived like a waterbird into the ocean. "But..." She was drowning.

Air finally found its way into her lungs. "I know you wanted a two-parent family for Daisy Ann. So...then I need a husband." A pause to take in more air. "I'll be on the lookout for one of those."

He seemed frozen. He didn't move. She didn't think he was even breathing.

"Weaver—"

He sprang to life, grabbed her hand in a punishing grip and hauled her from the room. Not letting go of her, he dragged her to the living room and drew her down to the couch.

In the soft glow of the room's lamps, he stared at her, his eyes hot and glittering.

And totally confused.

His ragged breath washed hot over her face. "On the lookout for a husband? What the hell do you mean by that?"

Her shoulders crowded against the sofa cushions. "Just what I said. I've not been in any big hurry to get married, but now—"

His mouth cut her off. It landed on hers with more

force than finesse. Her hands grasped his biceps, felt the tense tremble in his muscles. He wrenched away from her and ran a hand over his face, then raked both sets of fingers through his hair.

"Damn, Molly." Distinct distress sounded in his voice. "Damn."

He looked up, his face set. "You don't need to go looking. If you want a husband, then I'll marry you."

Molly's pulse jumped to warp speed. *"What?"*

"Doesn't it make sense to you?" He seemed calmer now, less agitated.

"But marriage for us?" Molly took a breath. "Now I feel like I'm forcing *you* into something."

He sighed, running a hand through his hair again. "No, Molly, you're giving me a solution I feel good about. A temporary marriage, Molly." He took a breath. "Then we can divorce and I'll give you custody of Daisy."

A temporary marriage. She hesitated. What choice did she have? "A temporary marriage," she repeated aloud, nodding.

"To satisfy the courts."

"To satisfy the courts."

He held out his hand.

She shook it.

They remained linked. After a minute, Weaver pulled her up and took her back to Daisy's room. Molly's stomach tightened again as they both stared into the crib.

The sound of Daisy's breathing filled Molly's ears.

Her heart swelled in her chest and tears stung her eyes.

One of Weaver's long fingers brushed the baby's head. "Jim had the same thin hair that she does."

The tears threatened to spill over, but Molly smiled, her stomach surfing waves of tenderness and nervousness. "I'm not sure it's quite the same. I think she'll have a full head of hair when she's a little older."

"Did you know her mother liked to draw? I wonder if Daisy has inherited that."

Molly swallowed, her throat going dry. "I'd like to hear everything about her mother and father. And I promise I will let her know how much she was loved by them." *And by her Cousin Weaver, even though he doesn't realize it.*

He turned to her, and the hand that had stroked Daisy's came up to make a rough caress against her cheek. "I know you will, Molly. I know."

Suddenly, something new charged the quiet atmosphere in the room. He half smiled. "I guess you're going to be my wife for a while."

Wife. Mother. Daughter. Husband. The words sowed a dozen flashing images in her mind. Her heart swelled again and she felt dizzy. "I guess I am."

He looked down at her, his blue eyes as dark as his hair in the early evening light. *"Molly,"* he whispered.

Wife. Husband. Molly's heart trembled. "Weaver."

Weaver's heart slammed against his chest as he walked Molly into the hall. He had found someone for Daisy Ann. The relief that had eluded him for weeks should untether him now, but instead of feeling free, he felt even more connected, and hungry for... something.

His hand tightened on Molly's, and in the darkened hall he stopped. "Wife," he said, the concept still puzzling.

She half smiled. "Hus—"

He didn't let her finish the word. His mouth came down on hers. She moaned, her lips immediately softening, her body leaning into him.

Blood rushed from his head to his groin, hardening him instantly. *This,* he understood. With his chest, he pushed Molly against the wall and slanted his head for a more forceful kiss. This kind of hunger he was familiar with. His tongue broke through the seam of her lips.

He dived into her delicious taste.

Molly welcomed him, her arms circling his neck, her fingers shoving into his hair, her hot mouth sucking on his tongue. He groaned, his body, impossibly, going harder. She tilted her pelvis against him, cradling his arousal, and he pressed back, trying to tell her how good this felt. How much he needed...her.

For tonight.

Just to ease this demanding hunger.

His mouth pulled away. He tried to start a sentence to tell her—

"Sh." Her fingers covered his lips. "Touch me. Hold me close. For tonight I want it all. Daughter, husband. Everything."

For tonight. That's all he needed to hear. With another groan, he took her mouth again, then slid his lips down her neck, while his hands found the hem of her T-shirt and slid up.

She arched, her breasts pushing forward into his palms. *Oh, Molly.* His fingers tightened, his mouth grazed her neck. Her nipples formed taut pebbles beneath the lace, and his trembling fingers moved to wrestle with the front clasp of her bra.

It was as bad as the lawn mower.

He took his mouth away from the distracting flesh of her neck, took a deep breath and fumbled again.

Smooth, Reed, smooth.

He couldn't catch his breath, or work his fingers, or get his heart to stop its crazy syncopation against his ribs. Another controlling breath, and his gaze flicked to her face.

Silver rims around pupils dilated by need. The want on her face grabbed hold of him, stilling his fingers, smoothing out the wicked beat of his heart. *For Molly.* She'd done everything for him.

This would be for her.

He smoothed his hands down her ribs and brought his mouth to hers again, kissing her, with control, with her needs foremost in his mind. A tender, gentle, searching kiss that he intended to soothe and incite and reassure, all at the same time.

"I'm going to have you," he told Molly, drawing her toward his bedroom with a light tug. She followed willingly, and he smiled. "I'm going to taste you, and feel you, and make you cry with wanting."

At the foot of the bed, he undressed her. T-shirt, bra, shorts. He left on her satin panties. He struggled to keep his touch gentle and reassuring. *This is for her, about her.* But his breath left him as his gaze ran over her high breasts, the tautness of her belly, her lean runner's thighs.

He pulled back the covers and watched her slide onto the bed, concentrating on the geometric pattern of the sheets to stop from losing it right there. He swallowed, hard, as her legs parted a bit and he imagined the mysteries of her sex beneath the innocent pale satin.

Weaver slid onto the sheets and, closing his eyes, reached out to bring her silken skin against him. He ran his palms down her back, his thumbs memorizing the fragile bumps of her spine. His fingertips found the elastic of her panties, slid under.

Warm flesh in his palms, soft satin against his knuckles. His breath left him.

He went to her mouth for more.

Hot lips that opened immediately for the instinctive thrust of his tongue. She tasted good, felt good, smelled like woman—perfume and sexual heat. *Desire.*

It clawed at him, urged him to go faster, but he held it at bay. *For Molly.*

He brought one trembling hand to the front of her body, let his palm slide up, bumping over each rib, until— Her breast fit snugly in his cupped hand, her nipple caught between two of his fingers. He bent forward, licked the tight crown.

She gasped, and the sound honed the already sharp edge of his desire. He licked again, then plumped her breast so he could suck her nipple strongly.

A moan, and then her fingers holding him against her. He transferred to her other breast, teasing her by tracing the edge of her areola with his tongue, then smiling against her perfumed skin when she pulled him closer to her.

Desire dragged him down again, with the taste of her breast in his mouth and the sensation of her hands beneath his shirt. She pulled at the material impatiently, and he broke away from her and tore the damn thing off.

Her hands dragged across his bare chest, and he closed tight his eyes, searching for control. *For Molly.* But his heart pounded primally, warning him how little he *could* control the feelings she brought out in him.

He pulled up one of her legs, wrapping it around his waist and rocking himself against her. She held him tightly, her mouth hot and wet against his neck.

No more control.

Weaver smoothed her leg away from him and quickly shed his jeans and boxers. He pulled a condom from the bedside table, put it on. One sweep of his hand dispensed with her panties, and then he hauled her up against him, bare flesh to bare flesh.

A shudder rippled through him. Her heat, his heat, her skin, his skin. His hand found the warmth and the wet between her legs. *Slick, for me.* His mouth found her mouth, entered. His body found her body, entered.

They were one.

The knowledge slammed him, and his heart somersaulted with the strangeness of it. Not Weaver having sex with some woman. Not Weaver finding pleasure in a woman's body.

But Molly and Weaver. Molly and Weaver rocking with desire for each other. Molly and Weaver, blood pounding, breath mingling, bodies *together*.

Molly and Weaver, one part of them moving in, one part of them moving up, arms encircling each other, legs entangling, mouths mingling. Every part of them together.

He heard their breaths come faster and faster. Felt the goose bumps of arousal washing their flesh. They silently clung, reaching... And in the instant before climax, Weaver opened his eyes.

Molly stared back, molten silver. As they hung on the edge, he felt them as separate beings again, the familiarity of separateness comforting. Then she clenched him, drew him invisibly closer.

Together again. And he slid farther into her body, farther into her, and they spun away into pleasure as one.

He came back to find himself crushing her to him,

his mouth against her cheek. He pulled oxygen into his lungs, then he tilted up her chin with his knuckle to see if she was yet breathing.

"You okay, sweetheart?" He dredged up a smile from somewhere, but assumed it looked as battered as he felt.

"Okay." She repeated the word as if it didn't have real meaning for her.

A chill ran through him. "I didn't hurt you, did I?" He pushed her a little away, took in the beautiful, disheveled state of her hair, the love bruise on her neck, the darkened shade of her nipples. "I didn't hurt you?" he asked again.

Her lashes swept over the cooling silver of her eyes. She smiled, her lower lip trembling. "Not yet," she said, her palm tenderly cupping his face. "Not yet."

Jonathon. Molly watched Weaver sleep and made herself dredge up another man's name. Jonathon, her ex-fiancé.

Her arms tightened around Weaver's neck in protest. But she had to make herself remember. *Jonathon.*

Hadn't she claimed her experience with him had made her immune to other "temporary types" like Weaver? Remembering Jonathon should protect her from the wild excitement she found in Weaver's arms.

She forced a long, deliberate breath into her lungs. *Don't panic.* A day of lows and highs capped off by the final...explosion of their sexual tension would do nutty things to anyone's emotions. Maybe all these scary feelings for Weaver were merely the aftermath of extremely good sex.

There. That's all it was. Good sex.

She concentrated on his powerful muscles beneath her hands and the lightly furred legs entwined with hers. Yes, all the pulse pounding and shiver producing could be chalked up to chemistry. Simple chemistry.

Male plus female. Yin and yang. Tab B into slot A.

"You awake?" Weaver's voice was slightly rough, same as the sensation of his palm sliding over her bare shoulder. "What are you thinking about?"

Heat rose up her neck on a direct path to her cheeks. It wasn't easy to look good sex in the face.

He leaned over and switched on the bedside lamp, and she drew away from him to shield her eyes from the light.

"Don't." He captured her hand in his and brought it against his chest. "Don't hide from me."

She stared at his hand holding hers, stared at the sculpted, golden nakedness of his chest. Beneath the skin, she imagined his heart pounding steadily, calmly, the same as it had pounded before she entered his life.

"Yin and yang," she whispered to herself. "Chemistry. Tab B into slot A."

"What are you talking about?" He grasped her chin and tilted her face toward him.

She met his eyes and tried holding on to her thoughts. "I'm thinking about good sex." Her blush reheated.

He chuckled, and she felt the rumble against her hand. "Yeah? So it was good for you?"

"Yeah," she whispered to the blazing blue of his eyes. Chills swept down her back, puckered her nipples. "And for you?"

"Damn good." He gathered her close and rested his chin on top of her head.

Against her chest, his heart pounded. *Ta-boom, ta-boom, ta-boom.* Maybe he wasn't so calm after all.

His big hand stroked her hair, and she turned her cheek into his neck. Hot chills raced over her again.

"It's not every day I go to bed with someone."

"I know," he said quietly. "Me, either."

Now what? Molly bit her lip. "Just for tonight" was all well and good before the big event, but what did one do now? What did she do when "just for tonight" changed in her mind to "just tonight's not quite enough"?

"I guess we went for option four after all," Weaver said.

Molly's heart squeezed and she slid away from him. "Yeah, I guess we did." She swallowed determinedly. "Remember what I told you about me and chocolate? I thought I'd do the same and binge myself free of you." She even tagged on a small laugh.

He blinked and looked taken aback. His hand rubbed across his chest. Then, finally, he waggled his brows in a mock leer. "So, how many tastes do you think it's gonna take? I'm only here for a while, you know. We should get started right away."

I'm only here for a while, you know. Inching back, Molly slid even farther from Weaver.

Jonathon. This time, his name came unbidden to her mind. Jonathon had taught her a lesson she was just getting around to remembering.

"How many tastes?" Weaver asked again.

Jonathon had made her unable to fool herself that she could ever change a man.

Her foot found the edge of the mattress, then air. She slid out of the bed, gathering up some of her clothes in a fist as she moved toward the hall.

"How many?" Weaver called to her.

She quietly opened, then shut the door. *Click.*

Jonathon—no, Weaver—had reminded her that temporary never changed to forever.

9

────→────

*F*ine, Weaver silently told the slowly changing numbers of his alarm clock. No need to wait for a decent hour. No need to pretend he was the slightest bit sleepy.

No need to miss Molly in my bed.

He'd wanted temporary, right? He'd wanted just one night.

But he'd wanted it more than just once.

He stomped out the need and tried thinking of business. Now Daisy was taken care of, thank God, and he'd get his attorney working on the papers tomorrow. That left only the house—realtor on that—and the stuff.

A lightbulb-brilliant idea flashed in his head. The stuff he could get rid of today by putting on a yard sale.

Not that it took much effort—heck, everything around the place was already for sale. All he did was open the garage door, round up a couple of catchy items from inside the house and spray paint a piece of scrap plywood with the words Moving Sale.

The street was alive with Sunday morning movement—walkers, joggers, people setting out in their cars. Two birds with one stone, he thought. *I'll stay away from Molly and rid myself of all this stuff, too.*

A lawn chair, the newspaper, a cup of coffee and he was set. He slapped on his sunglasses, lowered himself into the chair and proceeded to do his best imitation of a man unperturbed.

But his "perturb" level was a mile high.

"What's going on?" Molly came out the front door, Daisy Ann in her arms. She looked kind of perturbed herself.

"I'm getting rid of it." He waved a hand around the yard. "Everything." It would be just as easy for him to get rid of stuff as it was for her to get out of his bed.

Her eyebrows rose over her cool silver eyes.

An elderly couple walking by stopped and climbed up the sloped driveway.

He shot Molly a triumphant smile. "Just watch me wheel and deal."

The lady half of the pair wore a sun visor over her gray curls, and the male half had on a salt-water-stained fishing hat studded with flies. They went through the goods like old pros, the gentleman immediately gravitating to the tools Weaver had strewn across the lawn.

"How much do you want for this?" He held up the cordless drill that Weaver had used to fix the back fence. A shot of heat ran up his leg, a memory of

Molly's warm shoulder against him as he'd used the tool. Another shot of heat raced toward his groin as he remembered clutching both her shoulders the night before when he moved deliciously into her body.

He dropped the newspaper onto his lap and cleared his throat. "I can't sell that." The words popped out of his mouth.

The older man looked disappointed. "My nephew Dave could really use—"

"Sorry," Weaver said firmly. "I shouldn't have had it out here."

"Twenty bucks," the old guy said.

"No dice."

"Twenty-five?" The man still held the drill, *Weaver's* drill, in his hand.

Weaver rose out of his chair. "Sorry, sir. No sale." He took the tool from the man. "I'll just stash it away so no one else is confused."

He put the drill beneath his lawn chair and resettled in the seat.

"Yoo-hoo," called the man's visored wife. "The lawn mower doesn't have a price tag. What are you asking for it?"

Weaver's fingers tightened on the plastic arms of the chair. Not the lawn mower! He and the beast had an understanding now. "Uh-uh. Sorry, can't part with that, either."

"Fifty dollars, dear."

He shook his head.

A few more people joined the elderly shoppers. To

be safe, Weaver wheeled the lawn mower over to flank his chair. After a few minutes he had the barbecue on the other side, and then the set of barbecue tools joined the drill beneath the chair. All had received decent offers, but he just didn't feel the time was quite right to get rid of those particular things.

Suddenly, Molly's perfume curled around him. "You're a regular Monty Hall."

He breathed in her scent, savoring it. "None of these people are dressed up like pineapples."

She laughed. "So you'd sell if they were?"

No. But he didn't want to admit it.

He made himself get out of the chair and approach the older man in the fishing hat. "Anything else I can interest you in?" Weaver bent over, picked up a small appliance. "How about this?"

The man took it in his hand. It had a small square surface and an electrical cord. "I don't know what it is."

"Me, neither," Weaver answered. "Two bucks."

Molly came between them and snatched the item away. "It's a mug warmer, and it's mine." She shot Weaver a mean look. "Not for sale."

The old guy grinned as Molly stomped away, back to the house. "Word of advice, son. Check with the wife before selling anything."

Weaver grimaced. *She's not my wife.*

Yet, he reminded himself, and ignored the strange slide and bump in his gut at the thought.

The yard sale went downhill from there. He was

able to collect some money for a few items—he hoped to heaven they weren't Molly's—but a lot of the things seemed to have some relevant use for the time being.

Molly might need them.

Molly had touched them.

"Yoo-hoo! Yoo-hoo!" The visor lady's voice again. The older couple had stayed for an hour and collected a small pile of items at the bottom of the drive. "Yoo-hoo!" The woman and her husband emerged from the depths of the garage, each holding one end of a wicker cradle.

"How much for this?" She smiled, her visor askew with excitement. "My niece Andrea is expecting her first baby next month and—"

"No." Weaver barely recognized the hoarse and strangled sound of his voice.

The lady wilted. "Are you sure? Your baby is too big for this little cradle. This is for a tiny newborn."

"No." In a baby book were pictures of a just-born, doll-like Daisy swaddled in a blanket and lying in that cradle. The cradle was part of Daisy's heritage.

Like he was.

He threw away that thought and walked over to the couple, taking the cradle into his arms.

The lady straightened her visor, a disappointed expression on her face. "I understand, young man. You and your wife are thinking about another baby already, hmm?"

The old man chuckled. "Whether she is or not, I'll betcha he is."

The lady elbowed her husband. "Cut that out, Marv."

Weaver barely heard the banter. Right. Molly might want the cradle for her next child. The one she'd have with her husband.

Not her first husband, he hastened to remind himself. With her forever husband. He heard the front door open, then shut.

Molly again. She walked out alone, the baby monitor in her hand. Obviously Daisy Ann was down for her nap. She cocked an eyebrow at him, and he followed her gaze to the cradle.

"You'll want this," he said, holding it out. "It was Daisy's."

She smiled then, a tender, grateful smile, and took it from him carefully. He imagined her with that same smile, but her belly round and full with a child.

Some other man's child.

"Yard sale's over," he announced abruptly. He wasn't in the mood for it anymore.

He noticed, too late, that no shoppers remained in the yard. The elderly couple were halfway down the street, their meager items under their arms.

"Make a killing?" Molly inquired mildly, her gaze on the items he'd stashed safely by his chair.

"Yeah." From nowhere, anger spurted through him. Not from nowhere, he admitted, but from that image of Molly with a child, *not* his child, in her belly.

He dug in his pocket for the wad of bills he'd collected and held it toward her like a prized treasure. The money was proof that he was moving on. That everything, including everything between them, was temporary.

She looked over the money with interest, even prodding a couple of bills apart with a curious finger. "Way to go, big guy. Seven bucks."

Molly felt the heat of Weaver's stare as he followed her into the house. She carried the cradle, turning in the front doorway to be sure it wasn't nicked.

He dogged her footsteps all the way to the kitchen. "Seven," he said, disgust in his voice. "Seven lousy bucks. Four options, one baby, one dog. One woman who makes me absolutely crazy."

Molly hung on to her calm by her fingernails. After a night without sleep, the fingernails were getting pretty darn short.

"Your partner, Gabe, called during your sale," she said, putting the cradle down in a corner of the kitchen.

He flung himself into a kitchen chair. "Yeah? He didn't want to talk to me?"

She shook her head. "Not when I mentioned your stated intent to get rid of everything. He thought you'd be pretty busy."

He groaned, staring down at the measly wad of

crumpled bills in his hand. "Don't remind me. Does he want me to call him back?"

"No. He certainly is charming."

Weaver shot her a narrow-eyed look. "He's already a loser in the marriage department. Divorced."

Molly rolled her eyes. "Anyway, he told me to tell you that I'm better than Mary Poppins and that I'll make an even better bride."

Weaver groaned. "You told him about that, too?"

Unease wiggled down Molly's spine. "He asked me how you were feeling about giving Daisy up, and I guess I was a little excited. I told him about our arrangement."

He was silent.

"You haven't changed your mind, have you?" Her stomach twisted into a painful knot.

"No." He stared at the cradle in the corner of the room. "What about you?" A hand ran through his hair. "Our marriage could put your search for true romance on hold."

She swallowed. "Until our divorce, you mean."

"Right. We'll probably have to stay married for some time."

Funny, the idea didn't worry her at all. "I'm in no hurry. I told you that."

"Well, I don't see that we'd have to live together, really. Once this place sells..."

"We can move to my new house," she injected hastily. "It will be ready by the end of summer."

Couldn't the three of them be together for a little more time?

Weaver frowned. "You and Daisy certainly can do that. But I need to get back to Maryland ASAP. With fax machines and good luck, maybe I won't even have to return to California for the adoption proceedings or the divorce."

Molly bit her lip. "Oh, sure, and maybe we can get married by phone."

Weaver apparently didn't hear the irony in her voice. "Nah. We can go to Vegas for that."

Molly sighed. So much for any semblance of tender emotion in their agreement. "Guess I'll cancel the tuxedo and the wedding cake, then."

That caught his attention. His gaze found her, pinned her in place as she leaned against the kitchen counters. "I told you, Molly," he said, his blue eyes serious. "I told you what I'm about. I'm not a honey-I'm-home kind of guy."

Oh, I know what you're about, she wanted to say. *You're about caring for a little girl that isn't yours. You're about finding her the best life. You're about fulfilling a dream for me.*

You're about being hardheaded and tenderhearted, if you'd just admit it.

And speaking of confessions…

Molly realized she had one herself. Because at 10 a.m. on Sunday morning, in the warmth of the summer, in a stranger's house with an uncommitting man, she'd found love.

Her breath evaporated and her heart took a flying, fearless, feckless leap off the precipice she hadn't even realized she'd climbed.

I told you what I'm about.

Those six words—there's another number for you, Weaver, she thought in near hysteria—had brought everything to a head. What he thought he was and what she knew he was were so diametrically opposed.

What she knew he was, she loved.

What he thought he was kept them apart.

"Why are you looking at me like that?" Tension infused his voice. "What are you thinking about?"

I'm thinking how I want you forever. How I want to have Daisy as our little girl. "I'm thinking about—" She broke their entwined gazes and looked around wildly. "The—the cradle." *How I want to fill it with brothers and sisters for Daisy. Our children.*

The sound of his chair scraping back ran down her spine like a fingernail. He stalked toward her. "Don't mention that damn cradle."

She backed closer to the countertop, thinking fast. If Weaver pushed her much more now, she'd confess she loved him. Maybe lose him forever. But if she could show him how it could be with them...what love could do for them...

Her heart raced. She put her hands behind her, found the countertop edge, gripped it hard.

Weaver stopped in front of her. "Molly," he began, then broke off, shook his head. His hands came up and cupped her shoulders.

"Can a kiss be Windex to the soul?" she murmured to herself. Because that's what she wanted, needed. Weaver's mouth. A kiss. Maybe opening herself to him, giving herself to him would make him see.

Weaver shook his head again. "A kiss is the only thing you said that's made any sense to me."

To her, too. Maybe she could reach his heart with her love.

"Weaver," she whispered. Even through her T-shirt, the tile countertop felt cold against the heated skin at the small of her back.

"I want more, Molly. I can't get you out of my head."

She understood that. "I want you everywhere in me."

He groaned, his fingers flexed into her skin, and his mouth lowered.

She opened her mouth to him, invited in his tongue. He thrust into her, and his body pushed against hers, too, his arousal hot and hard and welcome against her stomach.

Molly's nipples immediately stiffened, and she rubbed them against his chest to ease their ache. Her arms pulled him closer, pulled him tighter to her. She wanted to melt around him, have him deep inside her.

He lifted his head and looked into her eyes. "See?" he said, his groin still pressing her, feeling good, yet feeling it was not enough. "See what you do to me?"

She almost laughed because he said it as if it might worry her.

His fingers ran down her arms to her waist, then insinuated themselves beneath her T-shirt. Hard fingers against her supersensitized skin. Her nerves ricocheting like lightning bolts.

"See?" he said hoarsely, pushing up her shirt. He found her bra, a stretchy athletic one without any clasps. He pushed that up, too, freeing her breasts, then ran his thumbs over her nipples.

Molly moaned.

"See, Molly." He said the same words again, but they meant something different now. He lightly brushed her nipples. "See how gentle I can be."

He took her mouth again. Possessed it with his tongue as if it were his own, as if he needed to be close to her in every way he could. Molly lifted his shirt and rubbed against him, bare chest to bare chest.

He groaned, broke away, and his fingers raced down her skin to the waistband of her nylon running shorts. "These have been making me crazy, you know."

Molly smiled, her whole body trembling with arousal and need. "I didn't know."

His thumbs hooked the waistband. "Every time I see you in them, I want to do this." He jerked them down, catching her panties at the same time.

He stared at her exposed skin, and Molly's heart hammered at the focused, tense expression on his face. "Molly, I have to have you," he said, his voice rough. "Let me have you."

He didn't wait for her reply, just fell to his knees and buried his face against her stomach, rubbing his prickly cheeks, one, then the other, over her flesh.

All the oxygen left Molly's lungs. She might die from pleasure, from sweet, erotic anticipation.

His tongue found her navel, swirled wetly inside. She moaned.

He trailed a path of kisses down her abdomen as his hot, big hands caressed her legs, moving from her knees to her thighs, gently forcing them wider.

Molly's breath came in shallow pants, and her body felt as if lightning had struck her skin. She was on fire, burning, and at her core she melted with the heat. *"Weaver."*

Couldn't he see? Couldn't he see what his touch did to her, what her heart felt for him?

"I'm getting there, honey." His fingers found the apex of her thighs, and she shifted, silently making room for them, but he skirted the hot center of her to move up and part her feminine folds. His mouth unerringly found its target.

Molly lost her voice, her reason, any hold on reality. She climaxed, her body helplessly tensing, one hand flexing in Weaver's dark hair.

He kept his mouth there while she trembled, gentling his kisses until her body quieted. He slid up her body and cuddled her against him.

She leaned on him bonelessly, releasing a long sigh.

He chuckled in her ear, kissing her cheek. "Liked that, did you?"

Tears stung her eyes, and she swallowed hard. "I liked it okay," she said, intentionally putting a smile in her voice. "But I want something more, something better."

He pushed away a bit and looked down at her with a quizzical half smile on his face. "I'm game, of course, but more? Better?"

She grabbed the neckline of his T-shirt in her fist and stepped away from her shorts and panties. She tugged him toward the bedroom. Oh, how easy it was to say in this context, "I want you."

The bed was rumpled and smelled like Molly's perfume and sex.

Weaver stretched and idly ran his hand down the length of her body, watching with relish as her nipples puckered and her eyes flew open.

"Daisy?" she asked sleepily.

He shook his head. "Still taking a nap, too," he answered, his gaze going to the nursery monitor on the bedside table. "Though why you thought we needed to grab this is beyond me. Not like we can't hear her bellowing lungs from a thousand paces."

"Thought our attention might be elsewhere." She scooted toward him to place a kiss over his heart.

The damn thing kicked up, racing against his chest.

He groaned. "You're going to be the death of me," he said, feeling the blood rush to his groin. His hand stroked over the long, loose fall of her hair. "I don't think I can do it again."

She eyed the evidence springing up between his thighs. "That a fact?" From the bedside table she grabbed a condom, and he helped her roll it onto him.

He groaned again, reveling in her caresses, then moved to pin her beneath him. He slipped easily inside, rocking softly against her. His eyes closed. "This is good, Molly."

Her pelvis tipped forward and he slid deeper. "Very good."

They made love again, like that, his gaze focused on her face so he could tell what pleased her.

Her silver gaze stared back, showing him her heart, her soul. What he saw there scared him, yet his body stilled as he felt himself become one with her again. *Together.*

He wanted to turn back, but her hands were on him, gently clasping him to her, and he wouldn't, couldn't, break the delicate connection.

Just as he couldn't stop the primitive satisfaction he felt when he watched her climax, or his own groan of release when he followed right after.

10

His body still in hers, his heartbeat not yet calming, Weaver kept his gaze locked with Molly's.

"I have to tell you," he said. "I tried it once before."

A haunted look came into her eyes. Tension stiffened her body. "I was there," she attested lightly. "Remember? About, um, twenty-five minutes ago."

"That's not what I'm talking about, Molly." She tried to wriggle from beneath him, but he kept her gently pinned.

"I need to get up. I want to take a shower before Daisy Ann wakes."

He shook his head. "I didn't want to tell you. But now I see that I have to." Looking inside her soul, he had seen what he was doing to her. How much he might hurt her if he didn't make her understand about him.

"You have a right to your privacy," she said, and bit her lip.

But that was fear talking, he knew. He didn't have any rights anymore. Not when he'd entered her silver heat. Not after he'd reached for that connection to her, then hung on to it as though it might save him.

"I should never have pursued you." He took a deep breath, thinking of all the would-haves, should-haves, could-haves. "I should never have let you get involved with me, knowing how you feel about family."

"Knowing how *you* feel about family." She was listening now.

"Yeah." He rolled off her but kept his hand at her waist. She had to hear him out.

With his other hand, he brushed her hair off her forehead, kissed her there.

A look almost of pain crossed her face.

"I'm sorry, honey." He cupped her cheek in his hand. "But I'm not going to do the family thing. I never am."

Her eyes closed briefly, then opened. "But why?" she whispered.

That's what he'd been waiting for. He was ready to tell it all, and she was ready to hear it. "You know my folks abandoned me when I was a baby. That I grew up in foster homes."

She nodded. "So you said."

He ran his thumb over the slope of her nose. "I don't know what you think about foster care, even how much you know about it, but I didn't have a good experience."

"I guessed that."

"It was the never belonging. Never feeling really

wanted. Moving on from one place to the next, from one set of so-called parents to the next.''

She stiffened. "People didn't hurt you, did they?"

He half smiled at her protectiveness. "Not physically. Not even intentionally. There are a lot of good people out there trying to provide for throwaway kids like me." He took a breath. "It's just that I didn't learn how a family operates. The support, the structure, the cooperation.''

She pulled up the sheet around her nakedness. "Well, if you realize that, why couldn't you learn?"

Here came the hard part. He tucked the sheet around her, as if he could protect her from the truth. "Remember how I told you that my cousin found me?"

"Daisy's father."

"Right. When he first married Daisy's mom, Jim came looking for me. He was excited about finding a blood relation. I'd just enlisted in the navy, and there he was, several years older, talking about the connection we'd have for the rest of our lives. He talked about his marriage, the children he planned to have.''

Molly bit her lip. "Poor Daisy to have lost him. He sounds like a wonderful man.''

"Yeah. He even got me thinking. So I'd been raised without family. That didn't mean I couldn't raise my own, right?"

Molly's eyes rounded. "Sure," she said. "Plenty of orphans and foster kids go on to have their own families. But *you?* I thought you'd always been dead set against a family for yourself."

He shook his head. "Not always. I was nineteen years old. I'd been thinking about Jim for months when I met Terry and Sam."

Wariness mixed with the surprise on her face. "Go on."

"Terry was older, twenty-five, and Sam was her son, the greatest four-year-old you ever laid eyes on. I fell for him instantly, and then for Terry. Sam's father wasn't anywhere around, and it didn't take me long to see myself as his daddy, and as Terry's husband. I wanted to marry her, adopt Sam."

"You'd found your family." Molly had the sheet up to her neck now, and she gripped it in her fists.

"So I thought." Even now, all these years later, the pain twisted in his belly. He touched Molly's cheek again and felt it ease. "But apparently Terry didn't think so."

"What happened?"

"I thought I was doing everything right. Sure, I had a little catching up to do when it came to holiday rituals and that sort of stuff, but I knew when I made the marriage proposal to Terry I should do it on one knee and with a big ring in my pocket."

Molly swallowed, and the color left her face. "So you proposed?"

"And she laughed in my face." The knot in his belly drew tighter. "Told me everything I should have known but didn't want to hear. That I didn't know anything about being a father or a husband. How did I think I could ever be a parent when I never had one?''

He paused to take a breath before repeating the most damning words. ''What did I know about love when no one had ever loved me?''

''Witch.'' Color flared on Molly's cheekbones.

A strangled laugh rose up in Weaver's chest. ''Thanks, honey. But while she might not have been tactful, I recognized immediately that Terry was absolutely right.''

''But—''

Weaver placed a finger over Molly's lips. ''But nothing. That's why I'm not taking any chances with Daisy Ann. Or with you. Both of you deserve to have the love that I can never give.''

Molly brushed Weaver's hand away from her mouth and swallowed around the lump of emotion in her throat. ''Now wait a minute—''

The phone on the bedside table started ringing. Weaver picked up the receiver, listened, then hung up almost immediately. He ran a hand through his hair. ''Well,'' he said slowly, ''there's some good news.''

Everything she knew about Weaver made her suspicious about how ''good'' the news would seem to her. ''What?''

''That was the realtor. Someone's interested in the house. *Very* interested.'' He rolled away as if he was planning on leaving the bed.

Molly panicked. "Hold it a minute. I want to talk—"

"Buyers for the house, Molly. No time for us to talk now." His face was tense, set.

She grabbed his arm as he kicked at the tangled sheets. "Come on, Weaver. Listen to me—"

"Honey, nothing you've got to say can change me," he said, the sad smile on his face making her want to kick him. "You know that. You've told me before you can't change a man."

Now she wanted to kick herself. "Weaver..."

"Thirty minutes, Molly. The potential buyers are going to be here in thirty minutes. They've been here before and want to see the house again."

"Thirty minutes?" Molly remembered her clothes strewn over the kitchen floor, looked down at her nakedness, then the destroyed bed. Thought about her destroyed hopes and dreams.

"This is all happening too fast," she said.

His feet hit the carpet. "Too fast?" He sent her another sad smile. "I've been waiting for this day for weeks. These people love the neighborhood. They want a house this size. It might be a sure thing."

"Might be a sure thing?" Molly murmured wryly. "There's a certainty for you."

He didn't appear to hear her as he gathered his clothes and headed toward the shower. "I gotta call Gabe and put him out of his misery. A quick sale and I'll be in Maryland and then we'll be back out in the field."

"What about Daisy?" *What about me?*

Pausing at the bathroom door, he shot her a wary look. "Like I told you, we'll get married before I leave. And then, the fax machine."

"Sounds like you're getting close to wrapping it all up." A numbness was settling over her. She couldn't quite believe how quickly her chance for love was heading out of her life.

"I am, Molly," he said quietly. "It's almost over."

The potential buyers really did appear interested. They'd arrived after Molly had hastily tidied up the kitchen and herself. They toured the house for more than an hour, had gone away to have lunch, and now they were back.

Molly sat unobtrusively in a corner of the living room sofa, Daisy Ann napping in her arms, Patch at her feet, while the couple inspected the house again. The wife was tall and slender, the husband bald and portly, and both so genial that Molly had to work hard to dredge up a dislike.

But they were taking away what kept Weaver close to her.

He was already slipping through her fingers. Excited by the couple's obvious enthusiasm, he'd placed a call to his attorney's home number and convinced the woman to go over some papers with him. It helped that the lawyer had been a good friend of Daisy's parents.

A wave of hopeless frustration crashed over Molly.

With quick fingers, she dialed Dana's number on the portable phone.

"I must have some sort of heartache wish," Molly told her friend. "I just discovered I'm in love with a man who is currently checking airline schedules for a one-way ticket out. What's wrong with me?"

"That's a loaded question."

"Seriously. First Jonathon, and now Weaver."

"How can you compare the two?" Dana scolded.

Molly stared down at Daisy Ann's sleeping face. "The fact that they both walked out on me comes to mind."

Dana's gusty sigh whooshed loudly over the line. "Weaver hasn't walked out yet, silly."

"Dana—"

"*And* you're getting married, *and* he's leaving his child with you. Even if he does get away, it won't be far or for long."

"Are you kidding? This guy thinks we can have a marriage by fax."

"Ew."

"Yes. But I need to stop whining and *do* something."

"There's a plan," Dana said.

"Yes, but *what* is the plan? Maybe this couple will hate the house." But in the distance she could hear them praising it to each other. She lowered her voice, though the words continued tumbling out. "I should never have cleaned the laundry room. Did I tell you

Weaver's a slob? Do you know that I fell in love with a man who can't sort laundry?''

"Calm down," Dana said.

"Calm down? Oh God, I'm not getting anywhere here. Maybe I should just give up on him.''

"You'll think of something," Dana said confidently. "And you know I'll always be here for you.''

Molly groaned. "Terrific. I guess only friendships last forever.''

"And true love." Dana's voice was fervent. "Alan proves that. With a little determination, true love lasts, Molly. It's worth fighting for.''

Chock-full of that determination, Molly cornered Weaver when he returned from the attorney's home late that afternoon. Daisy was cooing in her playpen, the potential buyers were gone—after ominous rumblings of an imminent offer—and Weaver was in the laundry room, of all places.

With the vague plan of confessing her love to him, Molly stood in the threshold of the small, white-tiled room and watched Weaver dump the contents of the dryer into an oversize laundry basket on the floor.

He gave her a quick glance. "If all goes well, this might be one of my last loads of laundry in San Diego.''

Scrap the confession. An annoying heat blossomed on Molly's neck. *I'm not baring my heart in a room with big appliances to a man who's counting down laundry loads.*

She took a breath, watching him toss a handful of dark-colored T-shirts into the plastic mesh basket. "Your meeting with the attorney went well, then?"

His arm disappeared into the dryer and he triumphantly pulled out a pair of green-colored jeans. "Great." He laid the jeans on top of the dryer. "She even wants to buy the two cars off me. She has a couple of teenagers."

A spurt of panic rushed through her. "But there are still so many other things around here that need to be cleared out. Furniture, the lawn mower, all the stuff in the garage." Her voice sounded normal, believe it or not.

He tossed another shirt onto the pile in the basket. "You have a lawn at your new house?"

"Well…yes."

"A backyard, right. Empty bedrooms?"

"Yes."

"Then all the stuff can go with you and Daisy." Now he pulled out a black T-shirt, held it against the jeans. With a frown, he let it join the other mishmash of items in the basket. "Anything you don't want you can donate to the Salvation Army or something. Perfect solution."

Panic flared again. "You really *are* in a hurry."

He didn't look up from the laundry pile. A blue T-shirt and a pair of shorts went into the pile of rejects. "This was all just temporary."

She wanted to scream. She wanted to stamp her

feet. Most of all she wanted him. "It doesn't have to be temporary."

He pulled a polo-style shirt, red, from the dryer and laid it on the green jeans. A pat signified approval of the Christmas combination. "What are you talking about?"

Emotion cracked her voice. "Decide you want to stay. Decide you want to be Daisy Ann's father forever."

He looked over at her, his eyes narrowed. "What the hell are you talking about?"

"Forever instead of temporary."

He froze. Long seconds passed, the silence sounding louder than Daisy Ann at her hungriest. Weaver didn't move, then finally he broke their joined gazes, slammed shut the dryer and grabbed up the garish outfit. He still said nothing.

Molly's nerves snapped. "Why do you *do* that?"

His head came around, and he stared at her.

"Why do you wear red and green at the same time? It makes me nuts. You had Daisy dressed for the Christmas parade the other day. Just avoid putting those colors together."

He laughed, though there was no humor in the sound. "I would if I could."

"What's that supposed to mean?"

"I'm color-blind, Molly."

"Oh." Her face heated. "Sorry. Guess you can't change that."

"Right. Just like you can't change me."

Molly swallowed, hard. Was that what she'd been trying to do? Oh, God. She closed her eyes. "Now I don't know what *you're* talking about." She tried that, for the sake of her pride.

"I know." Apparently he was going to let her get away with it. "One of the first things I found out about you was that you'd learned that lesson already."

Oh, God. "That's right," she said, turning away from him. "I did."

After a strained dinner, Weaver volunteered to put Daisy Ann to bed, and Molly did the dishes then sat down in the living room to lose herself in the newspaper.

She heard him come into the room but didn't look up. He stood silently for several minutes. Finally, he spoke. "They *are* silver, aren't they?"

She looked up. "What?"

"Your eyes. I can't distinguish many colors—I'm worst with red and green—but I'm pretty good with shades of gray."

"Yes, they're gray." She looked back at the newspaper.

"Silver." He crossed to the couch. Patch shifted in his spot on the floor to make room for Weaver's legs. "I thought maybe we could finalize some of our plans. About the wedding."

She froze. Wedding plans. She should be flying high, dancing the touchdown boogie when making wedding plans with the man she loved. Instead, her heart felt painfully heavy.

Don't give up. One last spark of hope fueled the thought. Molly took a breath and looked at Weaver. She slowly folded the newspaper. "All right."

He rubbed his chin with one hand. "Yeah, this is going to be good. I'm sure marriage will be the down and dirtiest way to push the adoption through."

"Down and dirty?" The spark sputtered out.

"Yeah. A quickie marriage, a quickie adoption, a quickie divorce. Then I'll give you full custody of Daisy Ann." He leaned back and blew out a sigh. "It may take a trip or two back to California, but I don't imagine you'll even have to visit Maryland."

The casual words pierced, then tore Molly's heart. *Quickie marriage?* She wouldn't even have to visit Maryland? Suddenly, the half dream he offered tasted sour in her mouth. "No."

His frown cut a V in his forehead. "No what?"

Her voice evaporated in the cottony desert of her mouth. She stood up and started backing out of the room.

"I can't do this." She choked out the words. She couldn't do a "quickie" marriage to Weaver. Not even for Daisy. Maybe especially not for Daisy.

"What are you talking about?"

"I want something real, Weaver." She backed into an overstuffed chair and held on to it for support. "I'm sorry, but I've just realized that." Trying to pull the ragged edges of her heart together, she paused.

He stilled, a wary expression frozen on his face.

He didn't want her. And she realized that she wanted a child *and* a husband.

No. Be honest with yourself, Molly. She wanted Daisy Ann and she wanted Weaver. The whole package or nothing. Because she and Daisy deserved nothing less.

She dug her fingers into the soft upholstery of the chair. "Daisy Ann needs a family. A mother and a father. Not some quickie. Not something down and dirty. She deserves clean and bright and lasting."

He closed his eyes for a moment and Molly rushed on. It was easier somehow with the blue gaze shuttered.

"You were right before. I *was* trying to change you." She swallowed to ease the huskiness in her voice. "But I just realized I won't get anywhere."

As if sensing her mood, Patch rose from his spot and came to her. She buried her other hand in the soft fur of his neck. "Just like I can't make you see colors, there isn't a word I can say that will make you see that you could be a father to Daisy and...something to me. Like I told you before, it's a feeling thing."

His eyes narrowed and his voice was hard. "You're leaving us, aren't you?"

"Yes." Despite her best effort, her heart started shredding again. "But please, Weaver..."

"What?" The word came out angry and harsh.

Molly took a step toward the front door, imagining the cool calm of the air outside this room. "Find Daisy Ann her forever."

11

Weaver stared at the bedroom ceiling and, instead of sheep, counted the ways Molly had done him wrong.

No more child care.

No more sharing of household tasks.

No more bright smile, dark braid, long runner's legs.

And the quiet. He blamed the quiet on her, too. When she'd taken herself and Patch out of the house two nights ago, she'd taken with her noises he would never have imagined he'd miss, like the sound of someone else showering while he made morning coffee, or feminine voices calling and cooing in a game of peekaboo.

"Hell." He flopped over on the mattress and slammed his head into the pillow. What he needed was a good dose of reality. His reality.

The bedside clock blinked over to 3:02 a.m. After 6:00 a.m. on the East Coast. He grabbed up the receiver and punched in the numbers for Gabe at the XNS offices. It was too early for his partner to be at his desk, but he could leave voice mail begging for a return phone call at the first opportunity.

"Yeah," said Gabe's real live voice.

Weaver held the receiver away from his ear and stared at it in consternation for a moment.

"Hello? Hello?" Gabe sounded tinny from this distance.

Weaver put the receiver back to his ear. "What the hell are you doing working at this hour?"

Gabe laughed shortly. "What the hell are you doing awake at this hour?"

"Looking for company, and I guess I found it. What's going on?"

"Looking for company?" Gabe echoed. "What happened to Molly?"

Weaver didn't want to talk about that, mainly because he didn't know how to answer the question. "Here one moment, gone the next," he said.

Their entire last conversation was like a puzzle to him. Her every word, her every look a piece that he had sorted and matched then rematched. No matter how he placed and replaced them, something was missing. The piece that explained everything.

"Dammit, Gabe, I might as well be nineteen again." Like the time when Terry wouldn't marry him. He felt just that confused.

And in ten times more pain, for some weird reason.

"You're an idiot, do you know that?" Gabe's voice was weary.

Weaver sat up in bed. "Why do you automatically think this mess is my fault?"

"Believe me, I know it is, just like I know you're going to go ballistic when I tell you why I'm at the office this early."

Weaver froze. "Yeah. Get to that."

"The Czech job. We've lost contact with Sonia and Harry."

Weaver slammed his fist into the mattress. "Dammit, Gabe. I knew they weren't right."

"Hold on, hold on. We don't know—"

"*I* know." He raked his hair off his forehead. "What's the colonel's plan?"

"I'm not sure yet. We have a meeting scheduled for 6:00 p.m."

"I'll be there." Weaver threw back the covers.

"We could use you, but if—"

"If you know me so well, Gabe, you know I'll be there."

"See you at six."

Pounding on her front door woke Molly. She sat up in bed, disoriented, still in a dream that included Weaver and Daisy Ann. Her heart frayed a little. Just a dream.

Another round of pounding. Who on earth...? It was four o'clock in the morning. Collar jingling, Patch rushed into her room and let out an urgent yip.

Molly belted her robe and jogged down the hallway, Patch at her heels. At the front door, she flipped on the porch light and fingered the curtain aside.

Weaver and Daisy Ann.

Molly's heart jumped to her throat, its beat pounding loudly in her ears. She pulled open the door. *Had he...had he possibly come for her?* Did he think now the three of them should be together forever?

He didn't waste time on niceties. "I need a favor," he said. "I need you to take care of Daisy for a couple of days."

Molly took in the overstuffed diaper bag at his feet and the house keys he held out to her. "What?"

"There's an emergency at work." Daisy Ann fretted, and he shifted her to a higher position against his shoulder. "Look, I wouldn't bother you, but I couldn't think of anyone else on such short notice."

She clutched two handfuls of robe to keep from snatching the baby into her arms. How she'd missed the little sweetie. She looked adorable, even with her pink jammies on inside out and a forest green cap atop her head. "So you just assumed I'd drop any plans I might have?"

He opened his mouth, closed it, opened it again. "Yeah, I guess I did." His expression turned from surprised to bemused. "I just knew I could count on you."

Well, that did it. Molly mutely held out her arms. And felt pleasure-pain as Weaver gently settled the baby into them. Lightning heat shot up her arm as he folded the keys into her fingers.

"I owe you one," he said, turning to leave.

You owe me my heart. A sudden thought dried her mouth. "Wait, wait!"

He stepped back to her, his eyes trained on her face. The gaze brushed softly over her, starting a round of shivers rolling over her skin.

"You said an emergency. Nothing—nothing dangerous?"

He smiled briefly, but it didn't brighten his eyes. "Not for me." He strode away, then paused at the end of the walk and turned again. Molly lifted Daisy Ann's little hand and helped her wave goodbye.

He closed his eyes, as if the sight hurt him, then moved determinedly away. "I won't be long," he called over his shoulder. "And then we won't bother you again."

Weaver wallowed in the familiar sights and smells of the largest of the XNS conference rooms. Coffee, inky and bitterly fragrant, paper, hot from the fax machine. Even the thick file folders had a pleasurable feel beneath his fingertips.

Geez, Reed. Pretty pitiful to get turned on by office supplies.

He ignored the jeering inner voice. He wasn't turned on, he was made comfortable by the return to his normal world. No diapers, no dogs, no talk about weddings.

Gabe slid into the chair beside him. "I see you made it."

"Just in the nick of time."

"Who's taking care of the baby?"

"Molly." Guilt gave Weaver a little jab. He saw her in his mind's eye, tousled and warm from sleep, her arms reaching toward him. Reaching for Daisy Ann.

That elusive puzzle piece floated through his consciousness again, but he couldn't quite catch hold of it. "Something's missing," he murmured to himself. "Something that explains everything."

Gabe shot him a funny look, but then the colonel seated himself and the strategy session began. Two operatives missing—they'd missed their check-in time by twenty-one hours now—and the assembled personnel had to plan a way to find them.

Eight pots of coffee later, someone rushed in. "Harry made contact. He got out. He's okay."

Pens were thrown down, laptops closed up. The colonel rubbed at his eyes with a gnarled hand. "And what about Sonia?"

"Sonia's dead."

Silence turned the room cold. Weaver made a fist, wanting to smash something. Though they all lived with death, worked with it day after day, each time its reality hit was like a baseball bat to the belly.

He still couldn't breathe right by dawn, when he sat in Gabe's office nursing another paper cup of bad coffee. "Damn it, Gabe. I told you. Someone else should have been assigned that job."

Gabe shook his head. "Sonia and Harry were just as good as you and I."

Weaver snorted. "Right. And now one of them is dead."

"It could have been you."

Weaver froze. His mind drifted to Molly again. Her hurt expression when he'd talked of the quickie marriage. Her bewildered expression when he showed up on her doorstep this morning. Her vulnerable expression when he'd said goodbye. "Nothing dangerous?" she'd asked.

She loves me.

His blood pressure zoomed skyward, heating his neck and setting his hands to trembling. He carefully set the coffee cup down on Gabe's desk. That explained everything.

She loves me.

The pieces of the puzzle he'd already possessed shifted, changed, reordered themselves. She'd wanted him as a husband, Daisy Ann as a daughter. The three of them together, forever.

And he'd suggested a quickie.

He tried throwing off the strange regret that held his heart. A quickie was all he had to offer, right? Temporary. Right?

"Right?" Gabe's voice broke into Weaver's thoughts.

"What?"

"I said, you can't be agreeing to anything dangerous until you've gotten things with Daisy sorted out, right?''

Weaver still wasn't thinking straight. ''Huh?''

''Well, it would be pretty lousy for Daisy to lose the only daddy she has.''

''She already lost her daddy.''

''And if she lost you—'' Gabe snapped his fingers. ''Boom! There goes another one.''

Weaver rubbed his hand over his chest. ''I don't like the way you're describing my demise.''

Gabe shrugged. ''Could happen.''

Could happen. Weaver's blood pressure rose a little higher. Even with Daisy safely ensconced in some nice family, he'd planned on being a part of her life, however peripherally. What if something *did* happen to him?

She would lose him.

He would lose her.

A dozen different images assailed him. Daisy giggling, crying, reaching, waving. In her crib, in the stroller. *In Molly's arms.*

''Hell.'' Weaver reached for his coffee cup and downed the contents in one scalding gulp. ''I must be losing it.''

Gabe propped his feet up on his desk. ''What's the problem, guy?''

And the puzzle shifted and changed once again, like a kaleidoscope. What just minutes ago had been orderly and complete now erupted into jagged, bursting shapes. A feeling, brilliant and intense, shot out from his heart to his fingertips and toes.

Weaver stared into the distance. "Maybe it's something like my color blindness," he murmured to himself. "Colors are there, it's just that I can't see them. And like that, I couldn't see my own feelings, though the feelings have been right there all the time."

"You okay?" Gabe sounded puzzled.

"I'm in love with them." Weaver raked back his hair and turned his gaze on Gabe. "Molly and Daisy Ann. I'm in love with both of them."

Gabe hooted. "Congratulations, you dolt! I could've told you that days ago."

Weaver crushed his paper cup and launched it toward Gabe's wastebasket. Two points. "And I think they love me, too."

Gabe sobered. "Now you just have to do something about it."

Weaver couldn't find them anywhere. He knocked on Molly's door again just to be sure. No response.

He'd already been to his place, but nothing looked lived-in. He noticed the grass had grown another couple of inches. He'd be mowing again soon. *Great.*

Where would Molly have gone?

Her car sat in the driveway, but he hadn't seen a sign of the baby jogger he'd left on the porch the day before. Out for a walk?

He shoved his hands in the pockets of his jeans. The sane thing would be to stay in one place and wait for her to come to him. He sat on her porch step, jumped right back up again, prodded by an urgent need to see Molly again. And his daughter.

The word sent his heart hammering nervously. Needing action, he set off down the street, hoping his instincts—and his love—would lead him to them.

Slowing to a jog, Molly grabbed the hem of her long T-shirt and blotted the sweat from her face. Why hadn't she done this days ago? Even though pushing the baby jogger and coping with Patch on a leash was awkward, completing two of her normal four miles was more soothing than retail therapy at the nearest mall.

She had three pairs of shoes, two skirts, a blouse and a dress to prove how ineffective that was.

She dabbed at her face again. She'd need a make-over next. Little sleep and a lot of sweat did not a beauty make.

In the block ahead, she glimpsed a man's figure. *Weaver.* Molly's heart twisted and hopped and she slowed to a walk. *No,* she thought. He would have called or something.

She squinted and caught a better glimpse before he turned the corner. *No,* she thought, pushing a wet lock of hair off her forehead. *I can't see him looking like this.*

Hot and sweaty would leave her vulnerable, and she needed all her defenses when she saw him again. When she had to say goodbye to Daisy Ann again.

Her heart squeezed, then twisted tighter. "Daisy," she whispered. In the shade of an overhanging tree, she stopped. Patch flopped down, ready for the rest. Molly spun the jogger and knelt to look into Daisy's face.

The baby grinned. Tears stung Molly's eyes. "Hiya, angel girl."

Daisy Ann blew a spit bubble.

"You won't forget me, will you? Because I'll never, ever forget you."

Patch whined and stood to butt his head against Molly's shoulder. She slung an arm around his neck. "I know, boy. She will forget us. But that's okay. Instead of memories, Weaver will get her the very best kind of family."

"A forever family."

She whirled at the deep voice over her head. "Weaver." She tried tucking a sodden tendril of hair into her braid.

"Hello, Molly."

There was something different about him. An inner quietness, a certainty she'd never sensed in him before. "Did—did everything go all right?"

His blue eyes darkened and he shook his head. "No."

She clung tighter to Patch. "I—"

Daisy Ann's squeal interrupted, and Weaver turned his gaze to the baby. He hunkered down, his knee bumping against Molly's ribs. She tried edging away, but his hand came out and gripped her forearm.

"Stay close," he said.

Stay close? she screamed inside, while he chucked the baby under the chin and made her laugh. Didn't he see she couldn't stay close? Not and survive.

He suddenly looked down at Molly as if he could feel her thoughts. With a hand under her elbow, he lifted her to a stand. "Let's go."

His hand slid down her arm to meet her palm. *Zowie.* His touch sparked off the familiar sexual burn. She tried tugging her fingers away.

He held on.

The walk back felt like a walk to the guillotine. *When I get there,* she promised herself, *I'll cut them out of my life just as cleanly.* She couldn't afford to prolong the hurt.

Weaver pushed the baby jogger to his front door. On the porch, Molly hesitated. "I—actually, none of Daisy's things are here. We've been living at my parents' the past few days." She didn't say that she'd wanted to avoid her memories of him by avoiding the house.

He made as if to turn around. "Then let's go—"

Shaking her head, she put her hand on his arm. "Please, Weaver. It would be easier for me if we said goodbye here. I'll drop off Daisy's things another time."

He didn't answer, just spent long moments looking down at Daisy Ann. Then he slowly smoothed his hand over Patch's coat. A wry smile came over his face. "I'm a coward, do you know that?"

"You?" She blinked. "What's a guy like you afraid of?"

He shook his head. "I thought you'd make it easy on me. Blurt it out when you first saw me. Let it spill on the way back to the house."

She stared at him. "What are you talking about?"

"I wanted you to tell me that you loved me."

Something had gone wrong with the world. Or maybe she'd taken too long a run. "Excuse me?"

"I wanted to hear those three little words first."

Trying to make sense of him, Molly looked from him to Daisy Ann, who was drooling, to Patch, whose tail was wagging, then back to Weaver. "I don't think I'm following you."

He shoved his hands in his pockets. A muscle jumped nervously in his jaw. "I'm in love with you, Molly."

She nearly croaked. "You are not." A choked laugh escaped her. "You don't know what love is. You told me that yourself."

A half smile turned up his lips. "But I think I do. It's wanting the best for the other person. It's knowing you can count on the one you love. It's hoping that *you* are the best for them."

Molly gulped, hot tears welling in her eyes. *What was happening?* Why did she feel so full of dread? She sank down onto the porch, resting her arms and her head on top of her knees.

She stayed silent for several minutes. "The world's all topsy-turvy," she finally said.

His big hand stroked her head and she heard wariness in his voice. "What do you mean by that, honey?"

"I'm the coward. After all my big talk about love and weddings and husbands and children, I'm afraid."

"Afraid of me?"

"Afraid of being hurt. Afraid I'll reach out for you and Daisy and it will all be snatched away."

He laughed without humor. "That's my line. I think I've always been afraid of being hurt, too. It's why I fought my feelings for Daisy and for you. It's why I let you leave us. It's why I was glad to be needed in Maryland this week."

Molly's heart beat loudly in the silence.

His hand stroked her hair again. "By the way," he said, "I've resigned from XNS."

She lifted her head. "You have?"

He nodded. "I've already called my old commanding officer who lives up the coast. He has a tamer type of security firm now and he says he has a place for me. XNS wasn't the right kind of job for a family man."

"Family man." She tried out the words. "I like the sound of that."

"What about the sound of this?" He paused. "Molly, will you marry me?"

Sunshine evaporated the fear inside of her. The tears warmed to sparkles in her eyes. "What?" A smile broke over her face. "I thought you said you knew to do these proposals on your knees."

He shook his head, certainty and happiness warming his grin. "And I don't have a ring, either. I just came with one thing in my pocket."

"What's that?"

"My absolute, certain, one hundred percent, forever love for you."

She threw her arms around him, kissed him, saltwater wet from those silly tears in her eyes. "And Daisy Ann?"

"I'm her forever, too."

Molly lifted her head from his neck and smiled at Daisy. "Did you hear that, sweetheart?"

She looked back at Weaver. "I love you." She held his dear, dangerously handsome face between her hands. "Say it to me once, will you?"

He laughed. "Say what?"

She whispered in his ear.

He laughed again. "Ready?"

She nodded, throwing out one arm to hug Patch to her.

Weaver rested one palm on Daisy Ann's head and curved the other around the cheek of the love of his life. "Honey," he said, quietly, seriously, because he meant it with all his heart. "I'm home."

* * * * * *

FANTASTIC NEWS!

For all you devoted Diana Palmer fans
Silhouette Books is pleased to bring you
a brand-new novel and short story by one of the
top ten romance writers in America

"Nobody tops Diana Palmer...I love her stories."
—*New York Times* bestselling author
Jayne Ann Krentz

Diana Palmer has written another thrilling desire.
Man of the Month Ramon Cortero was a talented
surgeon, existing only for his work—until the
night he saved nurse Noreen Kensington's life. But
their stormy past makes this romance a challenge!

THE PATIENT NURSE
Silhouette Desire
October 1997

And in November Diana Palmer adds to the
Long, Tall Texans series with *CHRISTMAS COWBOY*, in
LONE STAR CHRISTMAS, a fabulous new holiday
keepsake collection by talented authors Diana Palmer
and Joan Johnston. Their heroes are seductive,
shameless and irresistible—and these Texans are
experts at sneaking kisses under the mistletoe! So get
ready for a sizzling holiday season....

Only from **V** *Silhouette*®

Take 4 bestselling love stories FREE

Plus get a FREE surprise gift!

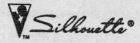

Share in the joy of yuletide romance with brand-new
stories by two of the genre's most beloved writers

DIANA PALMER

and

JOAN JOHNSTON

in

LONE STAR CHRISTMAS

Diana Palmer and Joan Johnston share their favorite
Christmas anecdotes and personal stories in this
special hardbound edition.

Diana Palmer delivers an irresistible spin-off of her
LONG, TALL TEXANS series and Joan Johnston crafts an
unforgettable new chapter to **HAWK'S WAY** in this wonderful
keepsake edition celebrating the holiday season. So
perfect for gift giving, you'll want one for yourself...and
one to give to a special friend!

Available in November at your favorite retail outlet!

Only from

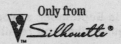